My Forgotten

Arbor Falls Book 1

MAYA NICOLE

Copyright 2020-2021 © Maya Nicole
All rights reserved.

All rights reserved. No portion of this book may be reproduced in any form without permission from the author, except as permitted by U.S. copyright law.

For permissions contact: mayanicoleauthor@gmail.com

This book is currently available exclusively through Amazon.

The characters and events portrayed in this book are fictitious. Any similarity to real people, living or dead, businesses, or locales are coincidental.

Cover Design by Mayflower Studio

Edited by Karen Sanders Editing

❦ Created with Vellum

AUTHOR'S NOTE

Arbor Falls is a reverse harem romance series. That means the main character will have a happily ever after with three or more men. Recommended for readers 18+ for adult content and language.

This book is dedicated to Bambi.

PROLOGUE

Ivy

I did it. Four years of undergraduate and two years of post-baccalaureate studies, and I was finally done with school. Ivy Taylor, Master of Environmental Science. It had a nice ring to it.

It had been a lot of work to get it done in six years, but now, at twenty-five, I was done with school and could start living my life and helping save the world at the same time.

"Ivy!" My best friend, Riley, came from behind me and wrapped me in a hug. "Congratulations!"

"I'm so glad you guys could make it." I returned my friend's embrace and then hugged her three men, taking the flowers Blake held out to me. "Thank you."

"We're proud of you, Ivy." Jax gave me a sincere

smile, and for once, I didn't feel like kneeing him in the balls. "It feels like just yesterday you were-"

"Jax, now's not the time for ridiculous speeches." Riley laughed and patted his chest. "Wait until we get to the restaurant."

Morgan slung his arm around Riley's shoulder and pulled her into his side. "I thought there was a party."

Some things never changed.

I rolled my eyes and looked around. "Did you see my parents?"

"I looked for them and texted, but they never responded." Riley bit her lip and shifted from one foot to the other. "Maybe there was really bad traffic."

I took my phone from my purse and turned it back on. I had three missed calls from my aunt and uncle. I frowned at the screen and returned their call.

I SAT down in my dad's office and looked around the space. When I was younger, he'd always let me sit on the small sofa and read while he was working. Now, the room was bare besides the desk and chair. They held too many memories for me to sell.

When I'd left for college, my parents sat me down and told me their wishes and explained where to locate important documents. I thought it was ridiculous, because who wants to talk about that with their parents when they're still so young, but now I was grateful.

I'd always known my dad had a locked drawer in his

desk, but figuring out where to find the key when I was younger had been impossible.

I took the key I found in the top right drawer of their dresser and unlocked the file cabinet drawer in the desk. It squeaked as I pulled it open, as if it hadn't been opened in a long time. I raised an eyebrow at the single folder inside.

Riley knocked gently on the partially open office door. "Hey, we're going to head out. We'll be back tomorrow at six."

I nodded, pulling the folder out and putting it on the desk. It wasn't very thick, but whatever was inside held weight.

"Are you sure you don't want to come stay with us for the night?" Riley pushed off the doorframe she was leaning against and came to stand by me. "That's all that was in the drawer?"

She put a hand on my shoulder as I opened the folder. I picked up the top piece of paper, and my hands began to shake as I read *Certificate of Finding of Unknown Child* at the top.

"What the hell?" Riley took the paper from me as my entire life flashed before my eyes. "Did you know about this?"

The paper had to be wrong. There was no way they weren't my biological parents. They had never said a thing about me not being theirs. Sure, I had red hair and they didn't, but the one time I'd asked about it in elementary school, they'd taught me about recessive genetic traits.

"No." I looked down at the next piece of paper, not

wanting to find out more, but needing to. "Why do I have a birth certificate with them listed as my parents?"

"I think that's what happens when you're adopted." Riley put the paper she was holding on the desk. "Is that all there is?"

Shaking my head in utter disbelief, I looked at the paper again and tears filled my eyes. It didn't matter, but if I really was adopted, I had deserved to know a lot sooner. Had they even planned on telling me at all?

I moved the birth certificate and found a newspaper clipping from the *Arbor Falls Gazette*. "This can't be happening." I choked on the words as all the information collided in my brain. I lifted the folder and shook it, hoping there was an invisible paper that would say it was all a sick joke. There were no other papers.

I was adopted. Twenty-five years old, and I was just now finding out my entire life wasn't even the one I was born into, and my parents hadn't bothered to tell me.

I handed the paper to Riley to read as my vision swam with tears. "Baby girl found abandoned in ivy bush outside clinic entrance. Anyone with information is urged to contact the Arbor Falls sheriff's office."

"Ivy... that's how I got my name. I was abandoned in a fucking ivy bush." I put my face in my hands. "Why didn't they tell me? How could they not tell me about something like this?"

Riley leaned against the desk and sighed. If anyone had some perspective on why parents kept important, life-altering secrets, it was her. "Would it have mattered if you'd known?"

I moved my hands and looked at the three papers. "It's who I am. I could have a whole other family out there. There could be genetic abnormalities or illnesses that I need to know about." I bit my lip to stop myself from bursting into tears in front of Riley. I'd drowned her in my tears enough already.

"You *could* have another family out there somewhere." She stood and then leaned down to wrap her arms around me. "But is it a smart idea to try to find them? Especially right now after losing your parents?"

Probably not, but what did I have to lose?

CHAPTER ONE

Ivy

I stood from my seat and held my shot glass in the air, the clear liquid threatening to spill over the rim. Maybe toasting with shots wasn't the best idea. "The last eight months would not have been the same for me without Richard. He's been the most reliable colleague and friend any of us could ask for. Cheers on your retirement, old man!"

Shouts and laughs went up around the table, and we threw back the tequila shots. I grabbed my beer and washed down the burning sensation as Richard began making his way around the table, saying his goodbyes.

When he got to me, he scooped me into a bear hug, lifting me off the ground before putting me back down. "Do you really have to retire? What am I going to do without you?"

"Probably get yourself into a whole heck of a lot more trouble." He laughed and squeezed my arm before making his way around the table to the other researchers and employees from our facility.

I had only worked for the Northern California Alliance Against Climate Change for eight months, but it felt like much longer. Richard was the chief engineer and helicopter pilot, flying us out to remote locations to collect soil samples for our research. His retirement left a gaping hole in the company. Qualified pilots with an engineering background were hard to come by. Especially ones that wanted to work in the middle of nowhere for chump change.

Originally, I had moved to Arbor Falls to figure out who I was after my adoptive parents died in a car accident, but I ended up falling in love with the town and the people, so I stayed.

I was no closer to figuring out why I was abandoned and by who. The town was less than five thousand people, but no one knew who had abandoned the gray-eyed baby with fiery red hair and a cry loud enough to make a man's nuts retract. I knew enough about genetics to know that my birth parents might not have had red hair themselves, but it still didn't stop me from staring at every single redhead I came across.

Our going away party wrapped up as the older members of our team left to go home to their families for the evening, leaving three of us—who happened to be the three youngest— to inevitably drink too much.

Reid slung his arm over Jessica's shoulder and

called the waitress over to our corner. "We'll take three more shots of tequila and another pitcher of beer."

Jessica let out a small groan and laced her fingers with Reid's. "I'm going to have such a bad hangover. Tequila is not my friend."

Reid and Jessica had been together longer than I had worked for Northern Alliance. At work, they kept it professional, but the second they stepped out the door for the day, they were all over each other.

Being the only three without families and under thirty, we typically hung out after work, either going to the gym, drinking, or hanging out at each other's houses.

Living in what I considered to be the country had taken some getting used to. I grew up and went to school in a small town off the coast of California, but everything was so close by. The small-town life of Arbor Falls had been a culture shock to me, but a good one.

Well, besides the fact they didn't have In-N-Out, which was unacceptable. I never told anyone, but I drove almost an hour one way a few times just to have it.

"There's a guy at the bar who hasn't taken his eyes off of you since we've been here." Reid's voice held a hint of a challenge as he passed out our shots. Reid and Jessica often tried to play matchmaker, rather unsuccessfully.

"I know." I'd felt him watching me earlier and had snuck a peek in that direction a few times. "I don't like picking up men in bars or coffee shops, you know that."

I drank my shot and chased it with a gulp of beer. I still could only feel a slight buzz. Everyone said they were jealous of my ability to drink the biggest male under the table, but really, it was a curse that had to be a twisted gift from my biological parents.

"I don't see a ring." Jessica glanced over my shoulder to the bar and then looked back at me with a grin. "You should go for it. He's pretty hot."

"Guys like him are either married or are at a bar just to pick up women." I admit, I was a bit jaded in the men department.

I braved a glance in his direction, and his brown eyes stared back at me before he looked down at his phone that was on the bar.

My breath caught in my throat, and I wanted him to look back up. He was the definition of handsome, with dark hair and tan skin. He seemed to be tall too, and his boots looked to be a good size—not that a big foot meant anything.

Had he been looking at me, or was it just a coincidence?

I put my forehead in my hand and groaned. "It's been too long since I hit on a guy, and that one looks like he's an ass kicker and panty ripper."

The stubble on the man's jaw and chin gave off a *don't fuck with me* vibe that put me slightly on edge but was also calling for me to investigate his allure. Not to mention the tattoos that peeked out of his dark-colored long-sleeved Henley and fanned across the top of his hands.

"You never know, he might be like one of those hot assholes you read about in your romance novels," Reid teased.

I threw a wadded-up napkin at him as I laughed. I didn't have the best track record with men. It was like I was cursed to find the most psychotic ones. But there was only so long a vibrator was a good enough lover, and I was at that point where I needed a night of passion with a man.

I finished my beer and pushed my chair back. The night was young, and I was getting tired of staring at the love birds canoodling in front of me. I loved my friends, but I always felt like the third wheel. There were only so many stolen kisses and glancing touches I could witness before the green-eyed monster reared its ugly head.

Besides, I wasn't one to back down from a challenge. It was as if it were part of my soul. If this guy was married or psycho, then I would never set foot in another bar for the rest of my life.

I turned away from the table and walked to the bar, sliding onto the stool next to him. He was still doing something on his phone and didn't look up.

That wasn't a good sign. A guy that looked at his phone more than the world around him raised red flags. He was probably on a hookup app, or texting his wife or girlfriend.

The bartender, Mike, approached. "What can I get

you?" He wiped the spot in front of me and put down a new chipboard coaster.

Mike should have known my order by then, but he still asked every time, just in case. "Two shots of your best tequila and your house beer, extra head if possible."

The foam seemed to help my body absorb the alcohol better. Really, it was probably all mental. My request often got weird looks, but also attracted attention and elicited *that's what she said* comments.

"I'll take the same. Put it on my tab." My neighbor spoke without looking up from his phone. His voice was slightly raspy and deep; it sounded like he had just rolled out of bed after a rough night of debauchery. It somewhat canceled out the fact that he was on his phone.

"Thanks." I tapped my fingers on the bar top a few times and casually leaned a little toward him, trying to see what was capturing his attention so much that he couldn't even look up from the screen.

He clicked the screen off and flipped the phone over before turning his head in my direction. "Sorry. I got a lead on a job." His eyes met mine before briefly glancing down at my lips.

Oh, damn. Was it just an accident he had looked at my lips, or did it mean he was interested?

"Are you new to town?" I asked, sliding the drinks toward us after the bartender set them down on the counter. "I haven't seen you around."

There were only so many bars in the area, and the same crowd frequented them.

"Something like that." He put his hand out. "I'm Cole."

I took his hand, which was warmer than expected, and it sent a shiver of excitement down my spine. I gasped and hid it by clearing my throat. "Ivy."

"Are we going to drink these?" He handed me a shot and grabbed one for himself.

I kept my eyes on him as we took the shots. It was bold to buy a woman drinks, especially when he appeared to be jobless. Top shelf at that.

"So, Cole, what brings you to Arbor Falls?" I traced the top of my beer glass with my index finger.

He watched my finger go around the rim for a moment before meeting my eyes. They were a caramel brown color and held an intensity that made me look away. The butterflies came at me in full force.

"Figured it was time for a change. Did you grow up here?" Geez, his teeth were so white I couldn't keep my eyes off his mouth.

"Just moved here eight or so months ago. I'm from Salinity Cove." I could have told him how I really was from Arbor Falls but was abandoned like a piece of gum in a bush, but that might have been too much too soon. "Have you had the chance to explore yet? There are some fun little shops and restaurants, and amazing hiking near the falls."

He took a drink of his beer as I spoke but never took his eyes off me. "I'll have to check it out. I heard there were wild animals though."

I shrugged. "They're more scared of us than we are of them. Last weekend we were hiking and saw a gray wolf. It was a rare sight since they aren't usually seen during the day. It watched us from afar but didn't come any closer. None of us could get our cameras out in enough time to take a picture."

"That's too bad. Are you sure it wasn't just a coyote?" He shifted closer to me on his stool.

"Pretty sure I know the difference between a wolf and coyote." At least, I hoped I did. Jessica and Reid both thought it was a wolf too.

His phone vibrated and he flipped it over so fast that I wasn't sure if I'd even seen it happen. He read the screen and sighed before picking up his beer and guzzling the rest of it down in one gulp. He wiped the foam from his lips with the back of his hand and stood.

"Sorry to cut this short, but I have to go." He grabbed his jacket off the hook under the bar top, sending a whiff of something spicy like cinnamon in my direction, and left before I could even get a word out.

I finished my beer in silence. Maybe it was time to delve into the world of online dating. I had heard of a few success stories. Perhaps I needed to try harder to find a decent boyfriend and have a real relationship. Surely there were more than a few single men in Arbor Falls.

I had dated my fair share of men over the years, but nothing ever felt right. I always felt like someone else was out there. I was picky, which was probably why I was perpetually single.

I stood to leave when Mike approached, smacking a

paper against his palm with an uncomfortable look on his face. "Your friend coming back?"

"No, he had to go." I raised a brow. "Why?"

He handed me a piece of paper that had a tab run up on it. My eyes bugged out of my head as I took in the long string of drinks and the final total. It was well over one hundred dollars.

Had he been drinking in the bar all damn day?

"You've got to be kidding me! You didn't ask for a credit card?" I'd frequented the bar enough to know the owner was strict on people skipping out on their tabs —if you were the last one from your party and no one else paid, you were stuck with it.

Mike gave me a look of pity before putting the empty glasses in a bin. "He paid for the first few drinks with cash and tipped well. He seemed harmless."

"I don't even know the guy!" Surely that counted for something. "I'll pay for the round of drinks we just had, but there's no way I'm paying for all of this. Who even drinks this much?" He'd probably been buying women drinks all evening.

"Pay, and the next time you see him, you can get the money back."

Mike was a little bit dense. Didn't he understand there wouldn't be a next time?

Mike cringed and then walked away. I'm sure I had a murderous look on my face. I'd pay it, since I could afford to, but I wasn't going to be happy about it. The alternative was Mike being stuck with it, and that didn't seem fair, even though he should have been a little less careless.

One thing was for sure, Cole was a dick.

CHAPTER TWO

Cole

It took everything in me to get up and leave the bar. I had been waiting for her all evening, and when she walked in, her scent had overwhelmed me.

Wolves didn't have fated mates or any of the bullshit that humans came up with. But I was pretty sure the female with the red hair that turned golden in the right light was my mate.

Fuck.

I held my phone to my ear as I walked to my truck. "You were right. She's definitely a wolf but doesn't smell like any pack from around here or even have that strong of a scent."

My pack became aware of the redhead about a week ago when one of my betas caught her scent near the falls. We had been digging for information ever since. We'd found out where she worked and that they were having a gathering at the bar, which was the perfect opportunity to see what her deal was.

Arbor Falls was neutral territory, meaning wolves didn't frequent the town unless the two packs on either side agreed to it. I wasn't about to let Silas know there was an unidentified female living in the town; that was asking for trouble.

About a half-hour drive to the south was a city of about one hundred thousand, where we did most of our shopping and business when we needed to. We were mostly self-sustaining, so it was rare I ventured there. I didn't like all the people.

To the north were mountains and campgrounds that humans camped in. Across a river, marking the northern edge of my pack's territory, were the falls where humans hiked. To the west was the WAP, short for West Arbor Pack, who had quite a few less than savory members, including Silas the alpha. We were best friends when we were kids, but then all hell broke loose and he changed.

Then there's my pack, the EAP, or East Arbor Pack. We kept to ourselves most of the time until our kind was at risk of being exposed. The redhead of unknown origin was a threat. All wolves knew to alert the local pack when visiting an area.

"From the information I was able to look up so far, it looks like Ivy Taylor moved to the area about eight months ago. A month before that, her parents died in a car accident on the way to her graduation. She works for Northern Alliance as a researcher," Eli, the pack's computer whiz and my best friend, explained what I already knew. "On paper, she's harmless. She's from Salinity Cove, and I'm working on getting her medical records. She's submitted her DNA twice to trace her lineage, but the samples weren't usable for obvious reasons."

I stopped with my hand on my doorhandle. "Harmless? An out of town wolf from somewhere that doesn't have wolves is not harmless, especially if she's sending her DNA to companies for testing."

"I agree. Is it possible she doesn't know she's a wolf?"

"How could she not know?" I shook my head. "It's possible she's sleeping with a wolf."

The thought made a growl lodge in my throat. No, that wasn't it.

"Maybe she's a loner." Eli sighed. "I'll keep digging and we'll talk tomorrow."

We hung up, and I slid my phone in my pocket. My ears perked up, and I ducked just as a fist came flying at the back of my head. It went through the side window, sending shards of glass tinkling to the pavement and all over the inside of the cab of my truck.

I swiped my foot out, knocking the assailant onto his ass, and dodged another punch from another attacker and sent him to the ground.

Wolves.

Their stench was enough to wake the dead, and I'd been so distracted that I'd let them sneak up on me.

I jumped into the bed of my truck as they got to

their feet and looked up at me. My wolf was clawing to get out, and I clenched my hands into fists. Shifting in town would spell disaster.

"Why are you here?" I spoke between gritted teeth as I looked down my nose at them. They were subordinates; I could tell from the way they backed away from me.

"A little birdy told us that your pack has been sniffing around town this week. Our alpha sent us to see why." The taller of the two took a brave step forward. "I imagine he's not going to be happy to hear *you're* here."

"This is neutral territory." Before I drew attention to myself standing in the back of my truck, I jumped and landed perfectly on my feet. "*Your* alpha is the one that couldn't come to an agreement."

The shorter wolf growled. "The town should be ours."

I growled right back, and they backed up into the middle of the street. There was no traffic since it was so late. "Tell your alpha that if he has an issue with me coming for a drink, he can send me an email. Or better yet, I'll email him about the window you shattered. I'm sure he told you not to be aggressive."

When I didn't see any behavior that indicated contacting their alpha made them nervous, I let out another growl that sent them running. Things had become increasingly more volatile between the packs over the years, and not from lack of me trying to ease the tension.

After using a rag to sweep out the glass on my seat,

I got in my truck, not surprised Silas had sent two wolves to rough up members of my pack. He never considered the wolf who would be slinking around town would be me.

~

I ROLLED over to the smell of food cooking downstairs and groaned. I tossed and turned all night thinking about her. Who was she? Why was she here? Why was her scent almost nonexistent?

And then I remembered my bar tab. Son of a bitch.

After a quick shower, I got dressed and went downstairs. I could smell bacon from a mile away, and my stomach grumbled.

"Morning, Cole." Eli stood at the stove frying cut up corn tortillas. "I hope you're in the mood for migas."

"Always." I poured myself a cup of coffee and leaned against the counter. "Did you find out anything new about the woman?"

"Her name is Ivy." I didn't need his reminder of her name. I wanted him to think I needed a reminder because he could usually see right through me. "I hacked into the county records office where her birth certificate was issued. She was adopted from here."

I watched as he poured scrambled egg over the fried tortilla strips. My mouth watered and I licked my lips. "Where exactly?"

"I did a little bit of digging, but she was abandoned outside the Arbor Falls medical clinic. There's no record of her birth parents." He turned off the oven. "Mind getting the bacon out?"

"Are you giving me an order?" I grabbed the potholders and laughed as he paled at my remark. "Don't get your panties in a twist. You should be used to me joking by now."

"Well, I'm not. You're my alpha. It was one thing when your father was still in charge, but now you should be treating me as your subordinate." Eli had been increasingly vocal about me treating him more like an omega, but I found the whole hierarchy thing antiquated. Well, at least in my human form.

I clapped him on the shoulder and opened the oven to pull out the foil-lined cookie sheet. "Fuck, I love bacon."

I grabbed a plate already on the counter and took half of the bacon, which got me a sigh of frustration from Eli because I was supposed to take most of it.

"Sure, just ignore what I said. As usual." He scooped the corn tortilla and egg goodness onto my plate.

He made himself a plate and sat down across from me at the kitchen table that overlooked the backyard. The sun was just starting to rise, and I had a busy day ahead of me.

I ate most of my food before sharing my big news with him. "I'm going back to Arbor Falls in a bit. I have an interview," I said, just as Eli took a bite of food.

He coughed as he swallowed. "What?"

"I put your numbers down for all the references and left a copy of the resume I submitted so you know who you are for each of the calls." I took a sip of my coffee as he continued to cough. "You all right?"

"A job? But... huh?"

I smiled at the curl to his lip and his furrowed brows. "Northern Alliance needs a helicopter pilot engineer guy. I overheard them mentioning they're hard to come by, and I figured I'd offer myself as a volunteer pilot until they find someone." I shrugged as his mouth opened to protest. "It's a way to get more information on the woman, and the facility is just outside the Arbor Falls boundary."

"How long has it been since you flew a helicopter?" Eli frowned at a piece of bacon he held in his hand before he pointed it at me. "What aren't you telling me?"

It had been a few years since I took to the skies, but it was nothing I couldn't handle. I assumed part of my interview would be to actually fly.

I finished my last bite of food and stood with my plate. "We need more information than what you can find online. She's doing something to suppress her wolf and I'm going to find out what she's up to."

"I hope you know what you're doing. The last thing we need is Silas's pack catching wind of you."

I decided not to tell him they already had.

CHAPTER THREE

Ivy

I slammed my car's door as I stepped out into the crisp March air. I was still in a cranky mood after Cole skipped out on his tab, which then became my tab. His name probably wasn't even Cole. It was possibly Jack, last name Ass. My faith in the male species was reaching a critically low level.

It was Monday, my least favorite day of the week. I liked sleep, and getting up and to work before the sun rose made me unapproachable for the first few hours. Add to that we had no pilot, and my mood was in the dump.

I opened the back door of my car and grabbed my bag that held my laptop, tablet, and cold weather gear. It might have been March, but taking soil samples from a high-altitude location got chilly.

I swiped my coffee mug off the roof and made it to the front door without dropping it. Win one for Monday on the books.

The receptionist greeted me with a smile. "Good morning, Ivy. Did you have a nice weekend?" Bless Stan's chipper mood every Monday. He had more than enough cheer to go around.

I grumbled at him with a small wave, and he chuckled. I guess the look on my face was enough of an answer.

Once I dropped my things off in my office, I headed to the conference room where we met Monday mornings to discuss recent developments and to go over any collection assignments for the week. The week would be light since our search for a replacement for Richard had gone unfilled.

We had known his last day was coming but had not found a suitable candidate that also held a passion for researching climate change. Richard had offered to stay on for longer, but we all knew he had a big trip around the world planned for him and his wife. Who were we to stand in the way of that?

I plopped down in my favorite chair—which was the same as all the other chairs—and sipped on my coffee as the others trickled in. We were a mixed bunch for sure. We ranged in age from twenty-five to sixty, with me being the youngest.

My phone buzzed, notifying me it was my turn in the word game I played with Jessica. I was beating her for a change, and I opened the app, examining the letters at my disposal.

Barbara, head of Northern Alliance, cleared her throat, ready to start our meeting. "I have some wonderful news to share. Yesterday, I interviewed a candidate for our pilot opening. He'll be with us on a volunteer basis until we hire a permanent employee. Let's give a warm welcome to Cole Delaney. He has an impressive resume, including a year as an aerial firefighter pilot."

What did she say?

My head snapped up from my phone to see *him* looking at me with intense eyes. He averted his gaze to look at Barbara. Jessica, who sat next to me, nudged me with her elbow, knowing exactly what I was thinking. I glanced across the table at Reid, who had a scowl on his face.

They hadn't been too happy Friday when he left me with a tab of over a hundred and fifty dollars. After Reid flipped out on Mike the bartender, he told us Cole had bought two rounds of drinks for a table of women earlier in the night.

Cole sat down in an empty chair at the other end of the table as Barbara continued with her updates. While swiveling back and forth in my chair, I tried to keep my attention on the meeting, but all I kept imagining was poking out Cole's eyes.

I was half zoned out, planning Cole's demise, when my name was said with an air of frustration, which meant it had been said several times already. Being caught daydreaming was embarrassing.

"Sorry. What?" I snapped out of my trance and scooted my chair closer to the table. "We should have these meetings on Tuesdays." The rest of the table laughed, and I even got a small smile from Barbara, who was used to my inability to function on Mondays. Luckily, she overlooked the minor flaw of mine.

"You and Cole will fly out at ten to collect a soil sample. I'll give you the coordinates after the meeting."

I bit down on my inner cheek to keep from cursing. She just hired him yesterday, and he was already going to fly? Had she run his fingerprints or called his previous employers?

"Has he had time to train with our helicopter?" Although it was pertinent to our research that we got a measurement, safety was also important. The last thing I needed was to burn up in a fiery crash right before my twenty-sixth birthday.

"I have extensive flight hours with various helicopters. Barbara and I flew yesterday, and I think she can agree my skills are more than adequate. From my understanding, this is a time-sensitive measurement, and I'm prepared to keep you safe." He kept his eyes on me.

I narrowed my eyes as he spoke as if he ran the place. He couldn't keep me safe if we were spinning to our deaths.

His accolades *should* have left me with high confidence in his flight skills, but something didn't sit right with me. I was unaware of proper helicopter pilot vetting, but it seemed awfully fast to let this unknown man fly an expensive piece of equipment.

I crossed my arms over my chest and turned my

attention toward Reid, who was discussing a new project he had started.

The room emptied once the meeting adjourned, leaving me with the questioning stare of my new colleague. If anyone should have been wary, it should have been me.

"Shall we address the elephant in the room?" I gathered my paperwork and stood. I needed to clear my mind before having to spend hours in a confined space, trusting him with my safety.

He rubbed his chin and frowned before standing and following me out of the room. "What elephant?"

"The one where you left me with a gigantic bar tab! I hope whatever ass you got Friday night was worth it." A few people lingered in the hall and their heads turned. Oops.

He followed me to my office. Shouldn't he have been doing preflight checks and figuring out the helicopter, so we didn't die in a crash? If I was going to die, I hoped it wouldn't be until after my birthday.

"I didn't mean to do that. I had an urgent call to make. Here." He threw three hundred-dollar bills on my desk as I sat down.

I gawked at the money in disbelief. He was unemployed—now a *volunteer* helicopter pilot—and he just threw money around like it was confetti. I wasn't an expert in spotting counterfeit bills, but it wouldn't have surprised me.

I looked up at him, meeting his stare that made my lower belly clench in a way it never had before. I really needed to find a man to scratch the itch because Cole

Delaney wasn't itch scratching material, despite how my body reacted to him. He'd probably give me an itch I didn't want.

Crossing my arms, I leaned back in my chair. "Make it five hundred and we'll call it even."

He raised his eyebrows before shrugging and pulling his wallet back out and throwing two more bills down. "I hope you tipped well."

"I always tip well." Why was I wasting my time talking to this guy? "With this kind of return on investment, let me know anytime you want to skip out on your bar tab."

"You're much more agreeable when you're drinking." He walked to the door before looking over his shoulder with a smirk. "We leave in an hour. You should get some more coffee before then; I think you need it."

This man brought out the worst in me. I bit my tongue to stop myself from blowing him a raspberry. I tried to act professional most of the time, but he made my blood boil to the point where I wanted to throw that out the window.

I wasn't sure I could trust a pilot that forgot things so easily, or one that was so cocky. Our multi-million-dollar helicopter was good, but nothing can outfly careless hands and a pilot that thought they were invincible.

After making sure my equipment was ready, I put on a thick flannel shirt over my long-sleeved top, a puffer vest, and grabbed my gloves and beanie before heading out to the tarmac with my research gear.

Reid and Cole were engaged in a heated conversation about some big mixed martial arts fight coming up. How could he have already forgotten what had happened three days prior?

Reid was a traitor. I had been hoping he would be a dick to Cole, but men never held grudges, at least not for long. Everything about this man was making my skin itch. Was it possible to be allergic to a person? It felt like it.

My eyes appraised Cole in his dark green flight suit. I had to give it to him; he was attractive as sin. I approached from the side, getting the perfect view of his thick thighs and rounded butt. He probably could squat a small horse.

I secured my gear in the back so it didn't slide all over the place. Reid held out my helmet and headset, which I took and let myself into the cockpit. Reid and Cole fist bumped before Cole walked around the front and climbed in.

"Perk up, he's not that bad." Reid leaned in and flipped a few levers before shutting my door.

I rolled my eyes and strapped myself in before shoving my head into my helmet. I rarely wore it, opting for the headset, but that day I felt it was necessary. Cole, on the other hand, put his headset on and gave me a quizzical look as if he didn't understand the need for the helmet.

He powered up the helicopter and started pulling forward to the helipad we would lift off from. He was experienced, so I tried to relax. I pulled my phone out of my jacket pocket and turned on some music, which I connected to the helicopter's main sound system. Hopefully it would prevent all conversation.

"You've got to be kidding me." His exasperated voice cut through the music as we lifted off in a northwest direction. "I'm *not* going to listen to this crap for thirty minutes."

He was referring to my late nineties pop playlist. I grew up listening to the songs since my mom was obsessed with boy bands. I cracked a smile and turned it up a little louder. Payback was a bitch.

He pressed a few buttons, and the music cut off. "I'd rather listen to nothing than that. You're going to make my ears bleed."

"That is quality music. You wouldn't know about quality though, would you?" I snapped.

"Reid said you were stubborn, but worth the effort. I'm pretty sure he's delusional. At some point you're going to have to move past my mistake. We're coworkers, whether or not you like it." He glanced in my direction before turning his attention back to flying.

A helicopter wasn't the place to argue, so I dropped the subject. "I'm cranky on Mondays, sorry." I scrolled through my playlists and put on indie rock, which was more my groove.

"Are you sure you aren't cranky all the time?" His laugh was teasing, and he turned up the music louder so I couldn't reply.

He had a valid point; my moods were worse lately. Especially with the crummy weather we'd had and not being able to get outside as much. Shortly after moving to Arbor Falls, I experienced cabin fever for the first time.

Growing up, I'd always been outside or playing sports. Living farther north meant colder weather, and the small-town environment meant less to do.

Something deep down told me I was exactly where I was supposed to be.

CHAPTER FOUR

Cole

This woman was something else. She was feisty and gave back tenfold whatever I threw at her. She wasn't a subordinate, that was for sure. The idea shouldn't have excited me as the alpha, but it did. But it also unnerved me because she should have known better than to challenge an alpha unless she wanted to wind up on her back.

And not on her back being fucked.

Damn. My mind went there, and now the image of her sprawled out naked, tits bouncing with every thrust, imprinted in my brain. She had nice, perky tits, a solid handful. I shifted in my seat, giving myself more wiggle room in my pants.

It was easy to steal glances her way since she had a damned helmet on and had no peripheral vision unless she turned her head. Talk about a blow to my confidence. A helmet wasn't a necessary thing during such a mundane flight. The sky was clear, the winds were calm, and we weren't dropping water on any fires.

I was already kicking myself in the balls, knowing that we were going to be landing in Silas's territory. The second we opened the doors, they would be able to smell me a mile away if they were patrolling in their wolf forms. Hopefully, we were far enough out from where any of them were.

We reached our destination, and I landed in a large open area between two expanses of pine trees. I powered down the helicopter and removed my headset. "How long will this take?"

She unhooked her seatbelt and glanced up at me. "Why? Got a hot date?" Was she flirting with me?

She took off her helmet, sending her scent in my direction. I shut my eyes and tried not to take a deep inhale. That would be creepy. I didn't want to be creepy.

What made the situation worse was she moved between the seats to the back, her ass brushing my arm. My eyes locked on target as she squatted down to unhook her bag.

Ivy was an attractive woman, and the jeans she wore hugged her body like they were a part of her. They were tucked into a pair of boots, and her green and purple flannel peeked out from under a black down vest.

I cleared my throat. "Do you need me to help with

anything?" Besides flying the helicopter, Barbara said I was to assist as needed once we were on the ground.

She shook her head without looking up from what she was doing. "A lot is riding on this collection. It's the last piece of data for a report that's going straight to the Climate Change Advisory Committee."

"Sounds fancy." I needed to research Northern Alliance more, so I didn't sound like a complete fool when she talked to me. I knew they were one of several facilities across the country that recorded environmental data, but that was it.

I exited the helicopter, walking around the front of it. The tree line was about two hundred feet away in all directions. I kept my eyes to the south, which was straight out the passenger side and where Silas's pack most likely was.

I opened the back door and held out my hand as Ivy stood with a tablet and a bin of instruments. She looked at my hand and then jumped down without my help. I blinked a few times and then dropped it to my side. The disappointment she didn't want to touch me was stronger than expected.

"How long have you been doing this?" I followed her as she walked about fifty feet while staring at her tablet.

She squatted down, putting her instruments on the grass that was starting to show signs of life again after the winter. "A while."

"A while? You're so young." I looked over her shoulder to see what she was doing, and she peered up at me, shielding her eyes from the sun.

"I'm almost twenty-six." She went back to her task. "You can't be older than what, twenty-seven?"

I snorted and scanned the tree line. "I'm thirty-four."

"You look and act way younger than that." I saw her smiling in the reflection on her tablet screen.

"I'm never going to live that down, am I? I really am a responsible man." Hell, I ran an entire pack. I shouldn't have rushed off like I had, but Eli said to call him.

I didn't understand why she hadn't picked up on my scent yet. Was she not a wolf? The possibility confused me, and I sniffed the air. Her scent was even stronger than it had been only minutes ago.

I squatted down next to her as she stuck an instrument in the ground and took a picture with her tablet. She removed the instrument and put the soil she collected at the end of it into a container.

"I'll be done in a few minutes if you want to go back to the chopper. You can brush up on your nineties pop so we can have a sing along on the way back." She couldn't be serious.

Rosiness bloomed across her cheek. "What's it going to take for you to forgive me for the bar?" *And why do you smell like a wolf?*

She sighed and took another instrument from the bin. "I hate Mondays, so it might just take it being Tuesday."

I laughed and stood, brushing invisible dirt off the palms of my hands. "Well, if that's all it takes..." I took a deep inhale as a faint smell of danger hit my nose. "Ivy. Get in the helicopter. Now."

Her back stiffened, and then she raised her tablet to take a picture of what she was doing. She lowered it slowly, setting it in the bin. "I don't take orders from men."

She pinned me with a glare. Her gray eyes smoldered with anger, but her scent had an acrid scent of fear. Did she smell the other wolves too, or was it my bossiness that made her scared?

My eyes snapped back to the trees and locked on where the scent was coming from. They were close, and in a few seconds two of them, the same two from Friday night, would be coming into view.

"Hurry it up," I snapped. So much for any progress I had made with her.

"You know, Cole. You're a real-" Her head raised to look at the trees as two wolves emerged. "Are those wolves?"

"Yes." She should have known they were. Could she not smell? Maybe something was wrong with her nose.

She quickly pulled the instrument out of the ground and put the soil in a specimen jar. She stood, her eyes still on the wolves who had stopped about fifty feet away. I moved in front of her and started backing up, pushing her toward the helicopter.

"What are you doing? I need to get the bin." She tried scooting past me, but I put out my arm, stopping her.

"This is not a fucking joke. Get in." My words dripped in warning. I didn't care if she had some deep-seated issue with men telling her what to do. She was in danger.

I corralled her to the helicopter and opened the door. "Get in."

She narrowed her eyes at me. "They're just wolves. They are more scared of us. It will take me a second." She darted past me and made a dash for her equipment.

Was she insane?

I pulled the gun I'd stashed in my flight bag and flicked off the safety. I didn't like to carry around a gun, but with Ivy being a question mark and me being out of my own territory, it was an added protection.

She walked back toward me, and her eyes widened. She had no clue that the two wolves were stalking toward us, their hackles raised and their teeth showing.

We were in their territory and they wanted blood.

CHAPTER FIVE

Ivy

I had never seen something so beautifully dangerous in my life. I'd seen a shark a little closer than I would have liked, but sharks didn't look like man's best friend.

I secured my bin as Cole stood facing away from the helicopter. He was fucking nuts if he thought it was a good idea to shoot at the wolves. I wasn't that knowledgeable about the laws, but shooting a wolf was probably against a protection law.

I was just about to tell him he was an idiot when growling caught my attention. It was stupid to take my eyes off the wolves in the first place, especially since they were now stalking in our direction.

A third wolf that was larger than the other two bounded from the trees and joined them. My breath caught in my throat. If wolves could talk, I was sure it would have been calling me all kinds of derogatory names with the stare it was sporting.

Its eyes were staring right at me, and it looked hungry.

My heart jumped out of my chest and into my throat. I had never seen a wolf up close before, and part of me was fascinated, but still terrified.

Cole walked out several feet and stared down the wolves who had stopped about twenty-five feet away. The bigger one was in front of the other two. How far could wolves leap?

Cole and the wolves were still staring at each other. It was almost like they were having a private conversation with only their eyes. I hoped he didn't get eaten because I didn't know how to fly a helicopter.

Cole fired two shots and sprinted for the door. The wolves were hot on his tail as he jumped in, slamming the door behind him. The wolves hit the door with what felt like the force of a small vehicle, and the chopper rocked.

Damn, those wolves had to be on steroids.

"Those fucking-" Cole didn't finish before the helicopter rocked again. "Son of a bitch." He slid into the front seat, powering up the chopper. "God dammit!"

Our first day together was going well, I would say.

I slid into my seat and put on my seat belt and helmet without saying a word as the blades stirred up dirt and debris around us. I could faintly hear wolves howl.

We lifted off, and I looked out the window as we rose into the air. The wolves were gone.

After a few minutes, I still heard Cole's deep inhalations through the headset, so I decided it was best to stay quiet. I was pretty sure I was in some deep shit after the stunt I pulled. He told me to get in the helicopter and I darted right back out into the path of the wolves. Barbara would write me up, maybe even fire me.

As we approached the research facility, Cole finally spoke. "Never do something like that again. It was incredibly stupid. Don't you know any better?" He took several deep breaths. "You told those wolves you don't respect their territory."

I took my helmet off as the wheels touched down and turned to narrow my eyes at him. "They are fucking wolves, Cole. I was getting soil samples. You're telling me they got mad because I collected half a cup of *dirt*?"

"You know that sound wolves make? A growl? That's a warning to leave. It was clear as day that those wolves were not happy we were there." He was speaking in a condescending tone, as if I were a child. "Then you stared the alpha down! To add insult to injury, yeah, you took their dirt."

He sounded like a lunatic.

"Let me guess, you're a wolf expert as well? Is that why Barbara so hastily hired you, or was it *something else* that got you this job? A little weekend romp, perhaps?" I probably crossed a huge human resources line, but my irritation was higher than it had ever been.

My suggestion struck a nerve, and he violently unhooked his seatbelt. "You almost got yourself killed! Two against an alpha and two others isn't good odds."

I laughed at his comment and looked at the gun lying on the floor between us. I quickly exited the helicopter after grabbing my stuff. I slammed the door and gasped, my hand making its way to cover my mouth.

The wolves had dented the cabin doors so badly I was surprised it had opened for me. Damn, I was going to be fired now for sure. The helicopter cost well over twenty million dollars.

Tears welled in my eyes, and I walked around the helicopter, my eyes on my feet so I wouldn't have to see Cole's glare. He just didn't understand how important this line of work was.

When I got to the back door of the facility, I stopped with my hand on the doorknob and braved a glance over my shoulder. The cockpit was empty, and Cole was nowhere to be seen. Had he run? If I were him, that's what I would have done. His first day and he was returning with a damaged helicopter. I should have run along with him.

Before I could investigate further, Cole popped back into the driver's seat and restarted the engine.

The door opened and Reid almost careened into me as he came out the back door.

"Jesus, Ivy!" He held his clipboard and followed the helicopter as Cole pulled it into the hangar.

They exchanged pleasantries before both began circling the helicopter. As they got to the passenger side cabin door, nothing registered on Reid's face. I had only stayed outside to watch Reid lose his shit over the damage. Instead, he slapped Cole a few times on the back.

Before either could notice me gawking, I slipped inside and made my way to my office, where I planned on hiding for the rest of the day.

∽

An hour had passed into my self-imposed exile when there was a swift knock on my door. Barbara probably had all the information now and had decided my future employment status. Damn it. I liked this job.

"Come in!" I looked back at my computer screen. Despite the past hour being a battle of my willpower not to fake being sick to go home early and the urge to cry, I had gotten a sizeable chunk of my report written.

I should have faked being sick.

Cole walked in, shut the door, and sat down in the chair in front of my desk. My closed door must not have been a big enough sign I didn't want to be bothered.

The tension hung between us as I continued typing on my keyboard, the clicking sound only minutely working to calm me down. At some point, I had started typing the same sentence repeatedly, just so I would have something to focus on.

A minute passed before he made a noise that sounded an awful lot like a growl. I stopped typing and looked at him. "Did you come in here to gloat that Barbara is writing me up or firing me over the wolf incident?" I steepled my hands in front of me as if I were the one in charge. "I'm curious to know what she will say about the gun you have on our premises."

"I'm not sure what gun you're talking about." His expression was blank, and the silence stretched between us once more.

I didn't know what I was up against. At first, I thought he was just a man that had a superiority complex. Now, I was getting the vibes that he might be dangerous.

"You know what? Here." I reached in my pocket and pulled out four of the five hundred-dollar bills he had given me. "Who the hell knows where this came from or if it's even real." I threw the money across the desk, half of it landing on the floor.

Someone needed to invent money that was easier to throw in anger; fluttering bills did not have the affect I intended.

"Thanks, I'll use this Wednesday at Morrow's." He quickly gathered the bills and left before I could speak.

After the door closed, I let out a frustrated grumble. Whoever had invited him to Morrow's for my birthday was now on my shit list.

CHAPTER SIX

Ivy

Wednesday night, I stood in front of my closet staring at my clothes. Nothing was really calling to me. I had been in a foul mood all week and just wanted to curl up on my couch with a container of chocolate chip cookie dough ice cream. Maybe I was PMSing.

Around mid-afternoon on Monday, I had ventured into Barbara's office to sniff out why she hadn't been by to see me. There was no mention of wolves, guns, or any damage to the helicopter. In fact, she said that Cole had told her I was the most professional and pleasant colleague he'd ever had. What the hell was his game?

When I had been sure no one would see me, I had snuck out to the helicopter hangar and examined the door. There wasn't even a scratch on it. I was either losing my mind or something fishy was going on.

My phone buzzed, snapping me out of my thoughts.

Jessica: *Pick you up in thirty?*

I had been staring into my closet longer than I had thought. I shot a quick reply before settling on a pair of faux leather, high-waisted pants and a purple shimmering top. The combo accentuated my waist and arm muscles. I quickly put on my favorite pair of strappy heels before going into the bathroom to do my eye makeup.

The only thing I had been blessed with from my biological parents was clear and smooth skin. I liked my red hair, but the Ariel comments and the question about the carpet matching the drapes had worn out their welcome.

I did a quick smokey eye, making my gray eyes pop, and brushed my hair out from my ponytail, letting it fan around my shoulders. The past few days it had looked more voluminous than usual.

I went down to the kitchen and took a quick swig from my tequila bottle. I was having enough issues getting myself out the door, might as well have a little help. Even if it had almost no effect on me, I liked to think it did.

My phone rang, and I picked it up while making my way to the door, grabbing my leather jacket. I would freeze a bit, but sometimes one must suffer to look hot on their birthday.

I was trying to forget that there was a real possibility that Cole had been invited. I hadn't asked Reid if he had because I'd been too angry.

"We're here, bitch! Get your ass outside!" I held my phone away from my ear as Jessica's loud voice assaulted my ear, along with loud music in the background.

I hung up on her, turned my porch light on, and locked the door behind me. I jumped in the backseat of Reid's SUV and laughed as Jessica handed me a flask. "Let's make this a night to remember and utilize our vacation day tomorrow to nurse our hangovers."

"Sounds like a plan to me." I had taken the two days left in the week off. I took a gulp from the flask, and my face scrunched in distaste. Jessica skimped when it came to spending money on alcohol. It was like she had no taste buds. "Ack! Reid, we really need to have an intervention for this girl."

Reid threw his head back and laughed, and headed toward Morrow's. It was our favorite bar that never disappointed in booze or liveliness. It also helped that they allowed drunken patrons to leave their vehicles in the lot overnight.

As we rolled into the parking lot, gravel crunching under the tires, my stomach suddenly knotted with nerves. I wasn't going to be happy if Cole showed up. He had taken up permanent residence under my skin.

"I hope you don't mind that I invited Cole. It will be nice to not play the third wheel to you two," Reid said as we exited the vehicle.

My worst fears were realized, and I stopped abruptly, staring after Jessica and Reid as they walked hand in hand toward the bar. I wanted to enjoy myself, not listen to another lecture about wolf etiquette.

Who did he think he was, the wolf whisperer? The encounter out in the field had been a one-time occurrence, and I'd probably never see a wolf *that* close again unless it was in a zoo. The thought of a wolf being in a zoo made me nauseous, and I shivered.

Just as I was about to pull open the Uber app on my phone and order a ride, the devil himself approached from the front of the building, looking like a delicious specimen of man. Cole and Reid did some elaborate handshake that men like to do, before all three sets of eyes turned in my direction. I was still standing in the middle of the parking lot, thumb poised over the app that would lead me to a warm bed and a pint of ice cream.

"Are you coming?" Jessica gave me a weird look. I couldn't blame her. I just hoped my face wasn't showing my true emotions in the faint overhead lights.

"Yeah, sorry, rock in my shoe." I casually bent my leg up and acted like I was picking a rock from between my toes.

With a sigh and a deep breath, I joined them, and Cole gave me a head nod before walking with Reid in front of us. He had even dressed up in dark wash jeans and a button-up shirt. He looked amazing, and that made me dislike him even more.

"What's your deal?" Jessica spoke in a hushed voice as she looped her arm through mine. "You look like you want to laugh, cry, and murder someone all at the same time."

"Reid shouldn't have invited him," I said quietly, slowing our pace a little so we'd be out of earshot. "He's bad news, Jess."

She laughed and hit me playfully on the arm. "He's harmless, silly. Plus, he's hot, and look at the ass in those jeans. If I didn't have Reid, I'd be all over that in a second."

I looked at her incredulously as something that sure as hell felt like possessiveness made my chest tighten. I glared at the back of Cole's head as we entered the bar. He had them all under his twisted little spell. Hopefully, they wouldn't be under it for very long.

The bar was busy for a Wednesday night—not that I usually went to bars on weeknights—and we found a table off to the side. Just as we sat down, Jessica and Reid both jumped up and declared they were buying the first round and left me alone with Cole. I had an inkling that they planned that.

As soon as they were out of range, I leveled a glare at him. "Why are you here?"

"That's rude. I was invited." He gave me a smug look, and I wanted to reach over and smack it from his face. He was toying with me now, and it was making me cranky.

I was usually a level-headed person, but something about Cole Delaney ignited a need in me to push back in the worst possible way. He was a big, walking question mark and the woman scorned part of me hated that.

"It's my birthday, try not to ruin it," I snapped.

He made my blood boil to the point where I felt

sweaty. I took off my jacket and put it on the back of my chair, aware that Cole's eyes slid from my face, down my shoulders, and settled briefly on my breasts before averting his gaze.

Jessica and Reid came back with beers and shots. I had lost my desire to drink but had to have at least one of the drinks they had bought. But one was never good enough.

The next few hours passed in a blur, and the alcohol slowly took hold of me. Cole was quiet unless Reid spoke to him, which was fine by me. I was starting to feel a strong buzz when two men walked into the bar. The hairs on my arms stood on end and my heart rate slightly increased at the sight of them.

In my inebriated state, I barely registered that Cole had silently stood and walked after them. I watched closely as they exchanged words. Judging from the tension in Cole's shoulders, the words weren't exactly pleasant. The two men turned and looked at me before leaving.

"That was weird as fuck," I commented to Jessica, who had her head on Reid's shoulder. She was done for the night.

"What?" She lifted her head up and then winced. She had tried to out-drink me again. She never learned; no one could out-drink me. "I think I need to get home before I vomit."

"Want us to order you a ride too?" Reid pulled out his phone and tapped on the screen. We lived on opposite sides of town, so it was cheaper to take separate rides.

"I'll take her home." Cole's voice held resolve, as if I had no choice in the matter. I looked at him and then back at his half empty glass of beer that had been sitting there for hours. I hadn't even noticed he wasn't drinking.

I'm not sure how it happened, but I must have zoned out because before I could express my concerns over my safety, Reid and Jessica were already out the door. I pulled out my phone, but Cole plucked it from my hands and grabbed my jacket and purse. The son of a bitch was holding it out to help me put it on.

I eyed him suspiciously and then slid my arms in. His fingers brushed over my collarbone as he let go of the fabric. I shivered and my nipples hardened.

Damn it. My body did not need to be reacting to him when I was drunk and in a needy state.

I followed him out of the bar, feeling more intoxicated than I'd ever been. I couldn't even walk straight and was confused at the feeling. "Just so you know, I'm only letting you give me a ride home because I'm too drunk to care." My words sounded slightly garbled in my ears, so I decided to keep the rest of my thoughts to myself. For now.

"Charming." He took my hand in his, and I looked down at our hands joined together. "Is this okay?"

"Yes." *No.* "Your hand is really warm." *I bet they would feel good running over my body.*

We walked a few blocks down the street before he opened the passenger door of a gray sports car. I stopped and stared at him slack jawed for a few moments before plopping into the soft leather seat.

"I thought you had a truck." I looked around the interior that was dark gray leather and had top of the line accessories.

"I do."

As he started the engine and pulled away from the curb, I glanced over at him. His jaw was set in a sexy scowl, and I was tempted to reach over and run a finger over his stubble. I had really had too much to drink.

"How did you fix the helicopter?" I'd almost been too scared to ask.

"It wasn't that damaged, I just banged it with my fist a few times and it popped back out. Sometimes when emotions are heightened things look worse than they actually are."

I was pretty sure I saw what I saw.

I rested my head against the headrest before shutting my eyes. The purr of the engine accelerating almost lulled me to sleep when my mind suddenly came back from alcohol fog and my eyes snapped open. I hadn't told him where I lived.

"Where are you taking me?" I looked out the window to see we were approaching the edge of town to the east. I lived to the south. "Let me out. Now."

He glanced over at me and then in the rearview mirror. "Do you see those lights behind us?"

I looked in the side mirror and saw a pair of headlights belonging to a truck. "Wow, another vehicle on the road at midnight, big whoop."

"Those are the two guys from the bar. They're

following us." We reached the edge of town, and the two-lane highway opened up into the great unknown.

Cole had his phone in his hand and was sending a text without even looking at the screen. That took major skill.

"You're crazy." I looked around, trying to spot my phone before I attempted to open the door. It remained locked, trapping me with a lunatic.

My heart pounded in my chest and I wondered if I would be able to fight him off when we got wherever it was he was taking me.

Cole suddenly accelerated to a blazing fast speed. I held on and looked back at the headlights that were keeping pace with us. The speedometer topped one hundred and was climbing. Maybe he hadn't been lying about the truck behind us.

"What the fuck is this?" A million thoughts and situations went through my head at once as I kept my eyes locked on the lights behind us which were still just as close.

"This is going to sound crazy," Cole said through gritted teeth. "But I'm kind of not supposed to be in Arbor Falls. And then there's you…"

He did sound completely crazy, but I had already determined that.

"Me? What about me?" I held onto the door for dear life as the scenery passed in a blur.

"You're... different." His knuckles were turning white as he gripped the steering wheel. "What are you?"

"What am I?" I was so confused.

I was preparing to give Cole a piece of my mind

when the truck behind us bumped the back of the car and caused my head to jerk forward. Cole remained in control, but the truck was right behind us again and rammed into us a second time.

The back of the car fishtailed, and my head cracked against the side window as the car rolled.

It felt like an eternity but was most likely only a few seconds. A scream refused to dislodge from my throat. I coughed as my lungs grew heavy. My ears rang, and my vision was tunneled before going black.

CHAPTER SEVEN

Eli

When Cole told me he was going back out after he got home from his "job" I about choked on the piece of steak I was eating. Cole wasn't one to go out. He wasn't even one to work, not in the traditional sense.

Cole was loaded and the rest of the pack wasn't too bad off either. Even if Cole wasn't a millionaire, he wouldn't have had to work. Alphas ran the day-to-day operations of the pack, especially since we had secrets that needed keeping.

I was lying on the couch in the living room reading when my phone beeped with a text, interrupting my peaceful evening of solitude and enemies-to-lovers epicness.

Cole: Two of Silas's wolves just came into the bar

and told me it was game time. I'm taking it as a threat. I already contacted Dante for reinforcements and I'm going to convince Ivy to come with me.

Dante was the lead beta of our pack and in charge of protecting the perimeter of our territory. If Cole had contacted him, that meant things were serious.

I turned off my eReader, put it on the coffee table, and stood to stretch. I'd been reading for way too long. I walked across the room to the floor-to-ceiling windows that overlooked the forest. The moon was bright in the sky and cast a silvery glow to the dark green of the trees.

Cole's voice came through his alpha connection, which meant he was far enough in our territory to use it. *"They're following us in a truck. I'm going to get as far into our territory as possible. Eli and Sara, be ready in case things go south."*

Sara was my twin sister, and we were the jacks of all trades of the pack. We were also the weakest wolves, with my sister ranking higher than me because I let her. She had enough to deal with without also being the omega.

I jumped into action, grabbing my shirt I had discarded earlier on a chair, and ran down the hall to the garage. I pulled on my boots before jumping in the extra-large SUV we used for medical transport. A row of seats had been removed and the entire back area was decked out with medical equipment and bars around the perimeter in case a wolf went crazy.

I backed out as soon as the garage door was open

and picked up Sara, who was waiting on the road at the end of a long gravel drive that led to my parents' house.

"Cute pajama bottoms. I bet all the ladies love the Baby Yodas." Sara put on her seatbelt and pulled her cellphone out of her bag, opening the tracking app that tracked all of our vehicles. "What did he take?"

"The Audi." I pulled out on the highway. It was just past midnight on a weeknight, so there weren't many cars.

"It's about five minutes away. They aren't moving so they either stopped or..."

"Crashed." I sped up, knowing time was of the essence. We had to be faster than the humans if they had crashed.

"They're off to the left." Sara gripped the *oh shit* handle as I cut across the oncoming lane and hit the dirt on the other side.

I grinned when she squealed and slowed down as we approached the mangled car, my grin quickly being replaced by a frown. It was worse than expected. A few of our pack were already on the scene, either with their own vehicles or they were hurriedly throwing on clothes we store as a precaution in trunks.

"I don't see them." Sara opened her door and the scent of blood and wolf instantly hit me.

Mine.

I gripped the steering wheel as my wolf pushed forward. "Shut the door," I growled.

She gasped and slammed the door shut. I wasn't an aggressive wolf, so a growl escaping was uncharacteristic. Even growing up, when we'd get pissed off at each other, we never growled.

I shut my eyes as another whiff of the female's scent hit my nose from Sara closing the door. A mate? There wasn't such a thing.

"Eli, what's wrong?" Sara tentatively put her hand on my arm and some tension left me. "We need to go help. I'm sure they're fine. Probably pretty banged up though, judging from the looks of the car."

I spotted the mangled car and gasped. A human wouldn't have survived a crash like that. Cole would have, but with injuries that would require a night of rest in wolf form to heal.

I nodded and jumped out before I lost my nerve. I could handle it, whatever *it* was. I grabbed my EMS bag out of the back and jogged to where Dante was giving orders as a flatbed truck pulled up to tow the car. The pack was a well-oiled, efficient machine.

"Where are they?" My question came out much more clipped than I'd ever spoken to another pack member.

Dante snarled at the interruption and then pointed to the tree line not far away. "He won't let anyone near her. He shut down my communication with him too. Maybe you can talk some sense into his stubborn ass."

Sara was already going in that direction. She'd probably used her nose, but I was trying my best to only breathe through my mouth.

I quickly caught up to her. "This might be a dangerous situation-" Cole's growl stopped us in our tracks, and I pushed Sara behind me. He was different in his wolf form than when he was human and might lash out at one or both of us. "Alpha, I'm going to need you to let us do our job. We're here to help."

He stood over Ivy's lifeless body with his body lowered, ears back, and his lips pulled back in a snarl. I dropped the bag on the dirt, not liking the way he was acting aggressively close to my mate.

"Eli, what are you-" Sara's voice faded as my wolf took over, and I dropped to all fours. "Son of a bitch! Dante, get over here!"

Seeing my mate lying in the dirt made me have more balls than usual, and I stalked forward, ready to fight Cole if I had to. His growling intensified, and he snapped his teeth in warning. He wouldn't hesitate to rip out my throat.

I lunged, and we met in a tangle as we rolled in the dirt. I fought my instinct to roll on my back and give him my belly. I got in one good nip to his hindquarter before he got me on my back and took my neck in his jaws. He applied just enough pressure to show he was serious.

In all our years, Cole had never forced me on my back before.

Out of the corner of my eye, I saw Sara rush to Ivy's side. She had blood in her hair, and her paws twitched. She was alive, but she was hurt badly.

I whimpered against Cole's hold on my neck, and he let go but kept his muzzle near my neck, snarling in warning before turning back to Ivy. I rolled over and then shifted back, rubbing at my neck.

I clamped down on my emotions that threatened to

spill over. Cole must have needed to take out his aggression. He had just seen a female injured right in front of him while he was driving.

He shifted as he knelt next to Ivy. He stroked along her muzzle and then looked back at me. "Are you going to help or not?"

Just as I grabbed my bag, she shifted, let out a pained cry, then passed out. I dropped to my knees next to her and began assessing the injuries.

"I'll pull the car closer." Sara jogged to the SUV as fast as she could.

"She's already healing broken bones and internal organ damage. I don't understand why she shifted back. Her body shouldn't have been able to shift in this state." I pulled a space blanket out of my bag and covered her. We were used to nudity, but having my mate be out in the open for anyone to see was not making my wolf happy. "What happened?"

"We crashed." Cole scooped her up off the ground and stumbled a bit.

I looked at his face closely. "You're injured, Cole." I tried to take her from him, and he growled. "You're going to drop her and hurt her even more."

His jaw ticked, and I furrowed my brows in confusion. He'd never acted this way toward me, like I was beneath him. I wanted to rip her out of his arms and claim her as mine, but this wasn't the time or place.

Sara pulled up next to us and opened the tailgate. Cole set Ivy on the blankets and climbed in. I grumbled because usually the only person tending to the wounded was in the back with them.

Although, typically, a wolf shifter who was injured as badly as she was, was still a wolf and not in their human form.

"This is... abnormal." I checked Ivy's pulse. "It's going to take longer for her to heal like this."

Cole stroked her red hair and didn't take his eyes from her pale face that was caked with dirt and blood. "I think that was her first shift."

I pulled out some alcohol wipes and began cleaning her face. "But that's impossible."

"I know." He sighed and took the wipe from me, taking over cleaning her face. "She partially shifted as soon as we stopped rolling and then kept shifting back and forth until she finally stayed in her wolf form. I moved her to cover in case humans got to the scene first."

"What happened to the truck chasing you?" I took Ivy's hand, hoping my touch brought her comfort.

"They didn't even stop." His head bobbed forward, and he shook it. "I need to heal. Fuck."

"I'll make sure she's safe, Alpha." I met his eyes and held them.

"If not, I'll kill you." He shifted and curled up next to her, putting his head on her stomach.

"You act like she's your mate," I whispered. That couldn't be. She was *my* mate.

Cole didn't react and shut his eyes. He passed out within seconds, his breathing becoming more even and deep.

A few minutes later, Sara backed into the garage and opened the tailgate. "Let's get her to the basement," she directed as she propped open the door into the house before coming back to the SUV. "Can you carry her by yourself?"

"The basement? I don't think that's really necessary." I scooped my mate up gently in my arms, careful not to wake Cole.

"Protocol. Just because she's a woman doesn't mean she isn't dangerous. And I'm going to go with she's dangerous. She just happens to show up in Arbor Falls? Yeah, I don't buy it." Sara started walking inside and then stopped, turning back to me. "She's a red wolf, Eli."

"That was her blood. Wasn't it?" I was so focused on Cole nearly ripping out my throat and the fact I had a mate that I hadn't really paid attention to her wolf's hair.

I frowned at the woman in my arms and cocked my head to the side, looking at her hair. It was a color that made me wonder if it was dyed, but the undertones were a coppery golden color. "Your eyes must have been playing tricks on you. Red wolf shifters don't exist."

I followed Sara inside and down into the basement. "You're right, though. With Ivy shifting erratically and us not sure where she came from, we need to secure her so she doesn't hurt herself or someone else."

Sara went to a cupboard and pulled out some clothes, setting them just outside the cage—which was more like a prison cell—I had set Ivy in. She threw a pair of sweatpants at me, which I quickly put on.

"Should we give her a blanket or pillow?" The

thought of my mate being uncomfortable or waking up on a cold floor made me want to punch something. I wasn't a violent person, despite being a wolf, and even my wolf was a lover, not a fighter. He was ready to throw all that out the window to protect her.

"She'll just tear them up if she shifts." Sara squatted down and began securing her legs with chains.

"We don't need to lock her up like that, Sara." I moved forward and her head tilted to the side. "I mean, if she really hasn't shifted before, she won't understand."

We utilized the cages for several reasons, including anything that would send a wolf into a craze. It didn't happen often, but when it did, we needed to be prepared, otherwise we risked exposing ourselves to humans.

The implications of humans knowing about us were severe. We would be hunted until every last one of us was locked in a facility or dead.

I turned away and took a calming breath. I wanted to rip my sister apart as she shackled Ivy to the floor, adjusted the space blanket, and then shut and locked the cage.

"I'll leave the key for the chains on the pile of clothes, okay?" She set the key down and gave me a stern look. "What's going on with you?"

"Nothing. I just don't want to see a female in pain."

Because that female was my mate.

CHAPTER EIGHT

Ivy

"Let's get her to the basement," a soft female voice said as my mind came back to me. I couldn't see or feel anything.

Oh, God. I really am dead. I was pretty sure the morgue was kept in hospital basements. Was this what happened when you died? You maintained some level of understanding as the last bit of light was sucked out of you? That was what it felt like.

I had to be dead. I was paralyzed and couldn't even move my pinky. If I wasn't dead, then I wasn't sure I wanted to live. The car had been going so fast. Could anyone survive a crash like that?

Pain ripped through me as if all my bones were breaking and my skin was being ripped to shreds. My mind went blank.

My entire body ached as I regained consciousness. It felt like I had been stuck in a clothes dryer with jagged rocks. My skin was hot and burned like there were a million tiny cuts everywhere.

Naked. I was naked.

I rubbed at my eyes as I uncurled myself, a whimper escaping. As my eyes adjusted to the dim light, my pulse skyrocketed. I was in a cell on a concrete floor with a thin silver blanket covering me.

I scooted toward the door, a heaviness weighing my arms and legs down. My breaths came faster as I yanked on the chains cuffed to my wrists and ankles. Acid burned my stomach as I considered what it all meant.

Kidnapped. I never thought it would happen to me as an adult, but who would? I would become another missing person no one knew what happened to. I didn't pray, but maybe I should start.

My eyes swimming with unshed tears, I crawled to the far side of the cage where I could barely reach through the bars. There was a pile of clothes, a sandwich wrapped in plastic, and a bottle of water. I ignored the sandwich, too afraid to eat something my kidnappers left me.

They wanted to keep me fed. What were their plans and did it include cannibalism?

As I grabbed the clothes, a key fell onto the floor, the clinking sound ringing in my ears. I stood on wobbly legs and tried to unlock the door, but the key wouldn't turn. A strangled cry escaped, despite my best effort to stay quiet. I was an idiot for thinking they would leave me a key to the door.

I started to panic, tears streaming down my face and blurring my vision. My breaths were shallow and short. I was going to be locked there forever. Did the guys in the truck take me or was it Cole?

I took the key from the lock and turned my attention to the chains on my arms and legs. I slid the key into the first shackle and it easily turned, the metal cuff falling to the floor with a clang.

The skin under the cuffs was red and raw, like I had been pulling on them for an extended amount of time. I quickly removed all the chains and slipped on the clothes that had been left for me.

The sweatpants and t-shirt were over-sized, but I wasn't complaining. I pulled on the gray pants and rolled the waist so they would stay up. The shirt fell to my mid-thigh but was soft and smelled like fabric softener.

Being clothed and unchained gave me new clarity and a tiny boost in confidence. I wasn't going to survive this if I gave up so easily and wallowed on the floor. I had a lot of life to live, Granted it would now be horribly twisted by the emotional scars this was going to cause.

I grasped one of the chains and yanked at it. It was bolted to the cement floor with two bolts. I checked each chain and sighed in defeat. The chains weren't going anywhere.

After closing the cuff on one of the chains, I grasped

it about a foot down. If I swung it hard enough and hit the right spot, maybe it would knock someone out. I really had no clue, but it was the best weapon I had.

Exhausted from everything, I sat back down on the hard ground. I looked around the basement, getting a lay of the land.

It was a large room that had three other cages like the one I was in. There was a door that was open on the far side that led into a dark room with security monitors.

My stomach rumbled, and I eyed the sandwich taunting me in its plastic wrap. Who knew how long I'd been locked there or how long the sandwich had been sitting there?

I grabbed it anyway and unwrapped it. When I breathed in, I was taken aback by how potent the individual smells were. Sourdough bread with roast beef and mayo. I was practically drooling as I took a bite.

What if they poisoned it?

I shook my head at the strange inner voice that sent a warning to me and took another bite. It tasted perfectly fine. If someone were going to poison me, they wouldn't waste perfectly delicious roast beef to do so.

I frowned at the sandwich as I swallowed another bite. They might have put sleeping medication in it, though. The thought made me swallow hard, and I threw the rest of the sandwich toward the stairs. That was sure to put a damper on their day if they stepped on it. I chuckled at the thought.

I was losing my mind.

Sitting in the quiet, besides the humming of the computers in the far room, was only making things worse. Something needed to happen. I could sit and wait like a sitting duck or give my captors a reason to come check on me. I'd rather be prepared for their arrival instead of caught off guard.

"Help!" I screamed with a hoarse squeak. *Crap.*

I took the chain closest to the door and started hitting the metal bars. My plan was to attempt to hit the person if they opened the door. I continued hitting the bars, the metal on metal sending shards of pain through my head.

I heard feet on the floor above. It sounded like hardwood and they were running. Whoever it was either didn't want me being loud in case the neighbors heard or cared about what was going on.

I quickly dropped to the ground, curling onto my side, facing away from the door with my weapon in my right hand. I dug in the pocket of the sweats for the key and held it in my left hand.

I wasn't sure how I was going to escape, but I was not one to give up. I was numb to just how much shit I was in and was in survival mode.

I clutched my stomach and moaned as if I had the worst cramps in the world. I wasn't sure how smart these people were, but they had to have some shred of humanity left in them since they had left me food and clothing.

The lock slid from its place and the door leading down into the basement was wrenched open. Footsteps pounded down the stairs. I kept my eyes clenched shut, not sure if I'd be able to go through with attacking someone if I had to watch them approach.

I moaned again and adjusted my grip on the chain. I hoped it looked like I was clutching my stomach in utter agony.

"Fuck." Recognition briefly fluttered in my mind but was swept away as I heard him unlocking the door.

I cried out, really putting on a show that I was a helpless female in debilitating pain. It was possible a career in acting was in my future. He stepped over me, and I opened my eyes, his black boots staring back at me.

Holy shit, I was going to try this escape thing, consequences be damned.

As he squatted down in front of me, I sprang up, pushing him back. Rage filled me, and I swung the end of the chain at him, not even aiming for anything in particular. Everything was a blur in my rage.

The cuff hit him in the stomach, and he grunted like it hadn't hurt him at all. My eyes snapped to his face and my breath left me.

No. Not you.

A deep feeling of betrayal coursed through my system that I couldn't explain. Cole was nothing to me, I barely knew him, but the fact that he was the one that had me locked up hurt my soul.

Cole's eyes flickered with annoyance as he blocked another swing of the chain. I was failing miserably but wasn't willing to give up, especially now that I knew he was one of my captors.

He snatched the chain and ripped it from my hands,

letting it fall to the ground. "I'm not going to hurt you, Ivy."

I let out a strangled half laugh, half cry and darted for the door. He was inhumanly fast as he blocked the exit. I managed to stop before running into him.

"I want to go home." My chin trembled, and I tried with all my might to keep the tears that welled in my eyes from spilling over.

"You are home." His voice held a finality to it that made the last surge of adrenaline pump through my bloodstream.

With a cry, I lunged at him with the key and scratched him across the cheek. I don't think it did much damage, but he stumbled back in shock, and I darted past him to the stairs.

I bypassed the sandwich, noticing he hadn't even stepped on it. I heard mumbled words from behind me as I climbed the stairs as fast as I could on weak legs. The oversized sweatpants were not helping.

Just as I reached the top of the stairs, I heard a grunt and a long string of curses. I looked back to see him shaking his foot at the bottom of the stairs. I never knew a sandwich could bring me so much joy.

I slammed the door shut and slid the bolt into the place, hoping it bought me time. Cole was muscular and pissed off now. He could probably kick the door down with no problem.

I was in a cream-colored hallway that had deep brown hardwood floors running its length. The setting didn't exactly exude kidnapper, but what did? I quickly decided the direction of all the light was my best bet; there were windows that way.

As I entered the living room at the end of the hall, the sound of the basement door smashing hit my ears and made my stomach drop. He was going to kill me. I knew it.

There were massive windows overlooking an expanse of trees. This was an expensive home, one that I would have totally been drooling over had it not been for a psychopath chasing me. I was like a magnet to them.

I skidded on the shiny floor as I turned and booked it to one of the doors leading outside. It was on the other side of the kitchen, which was massive and shiny too.

I fumbled with the latch on the sliding glass door at first, but was able to get it open and stumble out onto a deck before Cole had made it across the kitchen.

I bounded down the few steps and my bare feet hit the ground still frosted from the dew. I ran toward the trees not too far away. If I could just get there, I could hide.

My lungs burned as I sprinted across the side yard, past an outbuilding, and to the line of trees. There was no way we had crashed in a high-speed chase the night before. My lung function was better than when I played volleyball in high school and college.

I looked over my shoulder as I entered the trees to see nothing but the large cabin-style house. It was all dark wood, glass, and stone. It was breathtaking.

Where had he gone? Dread settled in at how alone I

was in this fight for my life, and I continued running through the trees.

My feet were frozen from the cold temperature and the moisture on the ground. I slowed to a fast walk and the adrenaline suddenly left me in a rush, almost dropping me to my knees.

Reality hit me like a ton of bricks; I had nowhere to run and no one would know I was missing for a few days.

I had to keep moving, but instead, I stumbled behind a thick tree trunk and slid to the ground. The bushes surrounding it gave some cover from the direction I had come.

Even if I did manage to escape, I was in a forest with no shoes or jacket. It was better than being stranded in the middle of the ocean.

I let the tears stream down my cheeks, the warm moisture sending small needles of feeling back into my frozen skin. I was so fucked.

Movement in my periphery drew my attention, and I pressed myself back into the tree as if that would hide me from the gray wolf prowling in my direction. It came slowly, with its head slightly down, its amber eyes locked on mine. I wanted to look away but was frozen, literally and figuratively. Twenty-six was shaping up to be a great year.

He stopped about five feet from me, cocking his head to the side while sniffing. The two wolves I'd seen up close on Monday were enough to last me a lifetime, but this one seemed to be more like a dog than a wolf.

People did have wolf dogs. Maybe he was Cole's pet

or belonged to the neighbors. He was beautiful, with gray hair covering most of his body and lighter hair around his muzzle.

He chuffed and trotted forward a few more steps. Why wasn't he attacking me? Did wolves attack if unprovoked? I knew you have to be careful with bears, but what about wolves? My college degrees did nothing to prepare me for this situation.

I tentatively reached my hand out. I was screwed anyway. If attempting to befriend a wolf was the last thing I got to do in my life, so be it.

The wolf ducked his head under my hand and let me pet the top of his head. He was soft and smelled faintly of fabric softener, which was odd considering he was a freaking wolf. Maybe he was a pet after all.

A growl came from my right, and I tensed as the wolf in front of me turned and let his own growl out. There was another, larger gray wolf stalking closer, and he *was* ready to attack. *Definitely not dogs.*

I pushed myself up and stepped away from them as they began to circle each other, their teeth showing. They were about to rip each other's throats out, and I wasn't about to watch that happen.

A small part of me urged me to stay, to do what, I didn't know. It wasn't like I was about to jump in the middle of two feral animals.

As soon as they lunged for each other, I ran back in the direction I'd come. If there was a house, that meant there had to be a road leading away from the place. Maybe I could make it to the highway and flag down a motorist.

The house came into view, and I ran across the side yard. It was such a big house, and had I not been trying to save myself, I would have stopped to appreciate how gorgeous it was.

As I rounded the side of the house, I stopped in my tracks. The car we'd been riding in the night before was sitting on a flatbed truck in the driveway. Well, what was left of it. It looked like an accordion. What the hell?

I should be dead.

I looked down at my body and then back at the car. It was so scrunched I couldn't wrap my head around how I'd survived it without a scratch. Had I been in the basement longer than a day? Even then, I should have been in a hospital, not able to run around.

One of the garage doors was wide open, and I looked inside. It was massive with five vehicles. My best bet was stealing one, so I snuck in. Of course, none of them had the keys in them, even though we were in the middle of nowhere.

I could have gone into the house and tried to find the keys, but I had no idea where Cole might be or if there were others. There was a shoe rack by the door leading into the house, but everything was men's sizes and would have just slowed me down. I'd just have to rip my feet up and deal with the pain and consequences.

The other side of the garage had a long workbench with tools hanging organized on pegs on the wall. I grabbed a hammer and exited the garage.

The house sat at the end of a gravel road that went

on for what looked like forever. I darted across the open area to the trees on the other side, hoping no one saw me.

I can do this.

Once I was far enough in the trees to be out of sight from the road, I jogged in the direction the road led. My feet hurt and my head pounded from lack of water and food. The few bites of sandwich didn't go far.

I slowed to a walk and gripped my hammer tighter. Every step I took crunched leaves and snapped twigs that echoed in the forest and sent a chill down my spine. Would the two wolves find me? Would Cole find me?

I came to another road that was narrower than the one I had crossed and looked down it. There was a house, and I nearly squealed with excitement.

I ran, tiny rocks and twigs digging into my feet, but I didn't care. I needed to get to a phone, so I could call the cops and this would all be over.

CHAPTER NINE

Ivy

The house at the end of the narrow road was a typical family house compared to the mansion I assumed was Cole's. It was in the same style —log cabin with stone—and had a big front porch that had a swing and a few chairs.

I ran up the three steps to the door and rang the doorbell repeatedly. My heart was beating in my ears, and I looked over my shoulder to make sure no one was following me.

A woman who appeared to be around my age opened the door. She pushed her glasses up on her head and her mouth opened at the sight of me. I didn't even want to know what was going through her mind, I probably looked like something the cat dragged in.

"I need help." I looked back over my shoulder again,

breathing a sigh of relief. "They locked me in a basement, and I need to call the police."

I might have been imagining it, but I swear a look of amusement crossed her face as she backed up and gestured for me to come inside. I hesitated because she was way too quick to just let me in.

"Are you going to come in?" Her dark brown eyes examined me again. "It might be better if you were out of sight."

She was right, and I was being ridiculous. I really watched too many movies and television shows. She was on the more petite side for being a few inches shorter than me.

I could take her, especially with my hammer.

Nodding, I walked in and she shut and locked the door. The front door opened right into the main living space. The furniture looked well-worn and comfortable, and the entire back wall was windows looking out onto a back deck and backyard surrounded by forest.

"I'm Sara." She walked ahead of me into the living room and picked her cellphone up from the couch as she flopped down. "Have a seat. You look exhausted."

I sat on the edge of an oversized chair as she lifted her phone to her ear, pushing her long, dark brown hair behind her ear. She seemed nice enough, but sometimes the nice ones were the ones you had to fear the most.

I held the hammer in my lap, unwilling to let go, even though Sara's eyes kept dropping to it. I didn't know if I'd be able to bash a skull in if it came down to it, but I could buy myself some time.

"Hi. I have a woman here who was locked in a basement." Hearing someone else say it out loud made it sound unbelievable.

Now that I was starting to relax, my entire body felt heavy, and I felt like bursting into tears. I was going to be okay. The police would come, and I'd be cuddling into my pillows soon.

She hung up the phone. "Can I get you anything to eat or drink?"

"You didn't give them the address." I stood and held the hammer in front of me. "Why didn't you give them the address?"

My heart fluttered in my chest and the hammer shook in my hand. I was panicking. Maybe stopping at the first house hadn't been such a good idea. It seemed far enough away that I thought it would be safe.

"Don't get your panties in a knot. They know the address from the number I called from." She pushed up off the couch and slid the phone in her back pocket. "We're pretty far out here, so it might take them some time to get here. I have some leftover stew in the fridge and some bomb ass sourdough bread if you're hungry."

Would someone that was out to hurt me want to feed me? Of course they would. Cole left me a sandwich in the basement. But this chick didn't know I was going to run to her house, so the stew couldn't have been poisoned unless she was a psychic.

I was about to decline as my mind raced when my stomach made the loudest grumble I'd ever heard from it. "That would be great. Some water would be nice too."

I had a nagging thought that something was wrong, but I brushed it aside. She wouldn't hurt me, and if she tried, she'd regret it. I had a hammer, and I wasn't afraid to channel my inner Thor.

I followed her to the kitchen, so I could watch her make my food. There was an island between it and the living room, and I sat on a barstool. I put my hammer in front of me as she pulled a glass container from the refrigerator.

"Our tap water is filtered on the way in from a well." She filled up a glass and handed it to me. "Nice hammer. Are you planning on bashing in some brains?"

I snorted and took a long drink. I hadn't realized how thirsty I was. "I grabbed the first thing I saw that I could use as a weapon. I should have taken the chainsaw."

She laughed, put the glass container in the microwave, and turned it on. "How did you escape?"

"I hit the guy that kidnapped me with a chain and then scratched him across the face with a key." I grimaced. I hadn't enjoyed hurting someone, even if he was an asshole.

"I bet that pissed him off." The microwave beeped, and she got the dish out without a potholder and placed it in front of me. Didn't it burn or was she just a badass? "Dig in."

I took a spoon she held out to me and started eating as she sliced a few pieces of bread from a loaf. It was some of the best stew I'd ever had. The meat was tender, and the vegetables and broth had so much flavor it was like an explosion in my mouth.

I'd just finished when there was a sound at the front door. The deadbolt clicked, and the door creaked as it opened. I dropped my spoon with a clang and knocked over the stool I was sitting on as I scrambled to get my hammer and move to the other side of the room.

"Ivy." Cole walked through the door with another man I didn't know right behind him. They were both without shirts and shoes, which was odd because Cole had on those things when I ran from him. "Let me explain."

I turned and ran, fumbling with the lock on the sliding glass door but getting it open just as a hand clamped down on my shoulder. I turned, swinging the hammer right at the other man's face.

He shrieked and let me go. In my panic, the hammer dropped to the ground, and I didn't bother picking it up. Time was too precious and both of them were in fantastic shape. They were muscular, but the type of muscles that held a lot of speed and power, not just strength.

I ran for the trees yet again. I felt like I was going to puke after the water and stew I'd eaten on a starved stomach. I should have known Sara was being too nice. Did the sisterhood mean nothing anymore?

I had to be in a nightmare. Had this been Cole's plan all along since meeting me in the bar? Maybe it was part of something bigger that Barbara was part of. You couldn't trust anyone these days.

My mind spun out of control as I ran. I couldn't hear anything behind me and looked back. I stumbled as my feet caught on a downed branch and fell forward, my hands taking the brunt of the fall.

Sitting up, I wiped my palms on my sweatpants. A small whimper made my head snap back the way I came. A female wolf—not sure how I knew it was female, it was just a feeling I had—hopped my way on three legs.

She sat down and stared at me with kind eyes. What was with all the solo wolves approaching me?

"Ivy." Cole came from behind some trees. I hadn't even heard him.

I scrambled away and got to my feet. The wolf had gotten up and then sat down again in between us. She faced Cole as he walked forward, and I backed into a tree.

He glanced down briefly at the wolf before she hobbled away with a gait that was half hop. Confused, I watched her retreat. It was possible I was hallucinating, and the wolves were a way for my mind to calm down.

"I'm not going to hurt you. I need to explain everything so you'll understand." He held his hands up in mock surrender and took a few small steps toward me. "This isn't what you think it is."

"Then what is it? Did we even crash? How long was I locked up?" I wanted to run again, but my ankle hurt from the fall. He'd catch me in an instant. "The woman called the cops. They'll be here any minute."

"Sara called me." He stopped and ran a hand over his face. "We crashed. It's Saturday."

"Saturday." I shook my head. "I was in a cage since Wednesday night?"

"Yes." He took another step forward and my eyes widened. He backed up again. "I'll stay right here."

I looked down at my body and then looked at him from head to toe. "How? We both should be dead. I saw the car in the driveway. Do you mean four or five Saturdays after we crashed? There's no way we could heal from a crash of that magnitude in two days."

"It's been two days. We aren't human. Let's go back to the house and I'll tell you everything, please." He watched me closely, ready to pounce if I tried to make a run for it.

"We aren't human?" I looked at my hands and then back at him. "Don't tell me we're mermaids." It was a weird comment to make, but my best friend was a siren and her three boyfriends were mermen... err, tritons.

His head cocked to the side and a small smile flashed across his face before he got serious again. "We are definitely not mermaids. Can we go back to my house so we can talk about this?"

"I think I'll just walk home. I could use the fresh air. We can't be that far from Arbor Falls." I stepped to the side and turned to head in the direction I thought Arbor Falls was.

Before I could get more than a few steps, he lunged forward faster than a rattlesnake and wrapped his arms around me in a bear hug, lifting me a few inches off the ground.

"Let me go!" I thrashed and kicked out with a leg but met solid muscle. It was like hitting a brick wall, and I gasped as a jolt of pain from my ankle spread up my leg.

He twisted me around in his arms, my hands going straight to his bare chest, and with a grin, he put me down briefly before slinging me over his shoulder like I weighed nothing. His arms locked securely across the backs of my thighs, and even as I flailed around, he didn't drop me.

"Put me down!" I pounded my fists into his back as hard as I could, getting a few grunts out of him, but not doing any real damage. I even tried open palm slaps, which just left red marks and made my hands burn.

He was stronger than expected and didn't seem to feel pain. I wouldn't go back to that basement if it was the last thing I accomplished in my life.

We left the cover of the trees and approached the house I had run to for help. *Sara.* I should have known something was up when she hung up the phone on the police.

I went slack over his shoulder, conserving what little slice of energy was left in me. My entire body ached, and bile was swimming in my stomach as I tried to calm my breathing down.

As we got halfway across the yard, my anxiety and fear bubbled over again, and my body was plagued with the pain of a million broken bones and fire. I had felt this before as much as I wished I hadn't. I'd just blacked out and couldn't remember what came after the pain.

I screamed and thrashed against Cole. My scream turned garbled and escaped as a howl as Cole lowered me to the ground.

"Fuck!" Cole backed up. "Eli! Sara!"

My body felt like it was being pulled in a million different directions as I rolled over onto my stomach, trying to crawl back toward the trees. I felt like I was outside of my body watching this tragic scene play out; A woman clawing at the dirt, trying to escape the muscled predator.

Two wolves appeared at the edge of the trees. One was the female missing a leg, and the other looked like the wolf I had petted when I had first escaped.

A final wave of pain took hold before an intense calmness washed over me, my body relaxing and warmth filling me. I heard popping behind me and jumped up on four legs.

Wait, four legs?

I was ninety-nine percent sure I was losing my mind. I had paws. I looked down at them and blinked. Had there been psychedelic mushrooms in that stew I'd eaten? Yes, that had to be it. Sara had poisoned me and now my brain was reverting to an ancestral state when we used to have hair covering our feet.

I felt something brush my butt, and I turned around quickly in a circle, trying to get to it. *A tail?* Okay, a fucking tail. And paws. Where was the *Jumanji* board? I needed to roll again.

One hundred percent sure I was having a break with reality.

I turned toward Cole, and instead of a person was a wolf, shaking shredded clothes from his body. Did he just turn into a fucking wolf? Did I?

I scrambled backward and looked down at the shredded clothes under me. I knew weird things happened to the body and mind when you panicked, but this was a whole other level of crazy.

Cole tilted his head back and howled, and the other two wolves did the same. I felt moved to join in, but the lucid part of me stopped me from doing so. Howling would be the icing on the crazy-town cake.

I took off, my instincts taking me to the trees on the other side of the property. Trees surrounded the whole house, but something told me that was the direction I needed to go in.

I heard the others behind me but tried to ignore them. I had a slight lead and was just as fast, if not faster than they were. I was a damn wolf and so was Cole.

Fuck.

I was battling with myself; the wolf part of me tried to get me to stop, but the human part of me urged me to keep running. The feeling was freaking me out, and I whimpered. The sound was foreign to my ears and sounded weak.

No more whimpering. Be strong.

My wolf had a mind of her own. *My wolf.* I felt that I could reign her in to an extent, but she tried pushing me out of my own head. I couldn't let that happen.

Oh, God, I'm going to be stuck like this. I'll never stand on two legs again. Never drive a car. Never feel a man's touch. Holy shit, I'm going to have to use the bathroom like a dog.

I was nearing a clearing that was just turning green after the winter. A scent hit my nose, and I stopped abruptly. Near the opposite tree line there was a deer standing in the path between me and another patch of trees.

It was beautiful, but not in a human seeing a deer kind of way. In a wolf seeing a meal kind of way. My entire body was attuned to it. I heard its breath that stuttered at the realization it was in danger. Its eyes widened, and its muscles twitched under its tawny coat.

It was frozen, its eyes locked on me and assessing its best hope for escape. The entire scene lasted a second. I tried to stop myself, but the wolf won, and in two giant leaps I didn't even know were possible for a wolf, I took down the deer.

Kill.

I bit down instinctively on the deer's neck as it thrashed beneath me, trying to escape. It was bigger than I was, but that didn't matter. I was the predator and my teeth ripped into it.

I tried to pull my wolf away from it, but hunger had taken hold. I feasted on poor Bambi until my stomach felt bloated. I knew without seeing myself that I was smaller than the other three wolves, and I'd probably just eaten what three of me could have shared.

My wolf was insanely satisfied. On a scale of cheap hot dogs to Japanese Kobe beef, the deer was a solid New York strip. I was disgusted at the thought.

I looked down at what I had done. It was an image I wouldn't soon forget. It had lost its life because of me. What if it had a family of little fawns? I was a murderer.

As my human conscience continued to beat me up, I

stumbled back from the deer, intense guilt threatening to send my feast back up. I plopped down heavily on my haunches and chuffed in defeat.

I felt a sudden pressure in my head and my body jolted forward as I shifted back to skin and nakedness. The chains and cage made sense now. I couldn't control this new part of me. A part of me I didn't even know I had.

I was a monster.

CHAPTER TEN

Eli

Cole might have been the alpha, but that didn't mean I had to agree with him. After the first night of Ivy being locked in the basement, I'd suggested we move her to the spare bedroom upstairs because if she really had never shifted before, the last thing we wanted was for her to wake up in a cage.

He said she'd be fine, and the cages were there for a reason. She'd shifted back and forth several more times, but most of her time was spent in human form. The impact of the crash really did a number on her. Plus, she was a red wolf, a rarity we didn't know the meaning of.

I'd just nodded as he listed out reasons she should be in the basement. He had valid points, but she was a female. How dangerous could she really be?

When she ran from the house, I'd followed her immediately. I had been working in the garden and smelled her fear as soon as she opened the door.

Her reaction to me in the woods was enough evidence that she had no clue about our world. Cole had already said as much after the encounter with two wolves during their helicopter trip.

How could a wolf shifter go so many years not knowing who they were?

We followed as she ran from my family's house. My face throbbed from her whacking me with a hammer. It was my fault for grabbing her when she clearly thought we were up to something nefarious.

She stopped in a clearing, and quicker than I'd ever seen any other wolf, took down a deer that probably weighed twice as much as her. Ivy was smaller than our females and thinner than a healthy wolf. She tore into the deer like it was the first meal she'd had in years. I drooled as the scent of the deer hit my nose.

I flinched and looked at Cole, who was taking in the image in front of us. She was going to make herself sick if she didn't slow down.

Cole stepped forward, and when I did the same, he growled. *"Stay back."*

I lowered my head and backed up, bumping right into Sara who must have just arrived. She gave me an annoyed look and then plopped down.

I sometimes wished it wasn't just the alpha that could communicate with each of us. It would be handy to have private conversations with my sister.

Ivy shifted back on her hands and knees, a gasp

coming from her. Cole shifted but kept his distance as she realized she had an audience and tried to cover herself.

Cole squatted next to the deer and looked it over before looking at Ivy, who was trembling. I wanted to go to her and comfort her, so I shifted back. Cole shook his head at me, but I ignored him.

"I said to stay back." He was pissed, but I didn't care. She needed someone, and he wasn't about to be that person. She was *my* mate.

"Are you all right?" I made my voice as gentle as possible. I squatted near her side and put a hand on her back.

She flinched away and stood, keeping her back to us. My heart sank into my stomach. She feared us, and I couldn't blame her for pulling away from me. I'd allowed her to be locked up.

Cole cleared his throat and gave me a look that made my balls retract. I was overstepping my boundaries by not listening to his command.

"I know this is scary and confusing for you. I wish I could have told you before, but I wasn't even sure what your deal was." His voice held a softness and sincerity he rarely showed.

"What my deal was? You did this to me!" She turned her head to look at him over her shoulder and glared. "I was perfectly fine until you! What did you do to me?"

He held his hands up and backed up a few steps. "Nothing, Ivy. You're a wolf shifter. You have been since birth."

"That's impossible." Her brows furrowed, and her

eyes looked up as if she was searching her memories, and then she laughed. "Is that why goats and sheep run from me? Or why we could never have cats?"

I snorted back a laugh, and she turned her glare on me. My stomach twisted, and I averted my gaze.

"What the fuck? We need to find out where she came from and who her parents are." Cole rubbed the back of his neck. *"She's also the most dominant female I've encountered."*

"My wolf wants to show her his belly and get a belly rub." I probably should have kept that to myself because it was going to cause trouble. It was one thing for me to be forced onto my back, but to want to do it *and* get a belly rub? My wolf had it bad.

Cole's eyes widened, and he stepped closer to Ivy, narrowing his eyes. "Who sent you?"

"Who *sent* me? You have got to be kidding me. You *kidnapped* me and locked me away, or did you forget about that already?" She turned and put one arm over her breasts and one over her southern lady bits.

I bit my lip to stop myself from smiling. I loved the way she wasn't scared of Cole and gave him sass he didn't know what to do with. Any other female would have been on the ground with his wolf at their throat by now.

Cole laughed and looked her up and down. "Nudity doesn't bother us. Soon it won't bother you either." He turned back toward the house. "Let's go."

She scowled at his back and followed a few feet behind him as we walked the way we had run from.

She turned her head back toward me. "You can walk in front of me."

"I won't look." At least I didn't think I would. I was a respectable wolf, not a horn dog.

"Listen here... What's your name?" She raised an eyebrow.

"Elias, but everyone calls me Eli. You can call me whichever you prefer." She could call me ass and I would be happy.

"Eli, I don't care if you say you won't look. I want you walking in front of me, eyes on your buddy's ass and not on mine. Got it?" Sara chuffed, and Ivy looked at her. "You too, I don't care if you're a female."

"Who's going to protect your back?" I moved in front of her. "Your back is the most vulnerable."

"I can protect my own ass. Thank you very much."

Cole snorted and shook his head as we made our way back to the house. It would have been faster to shift and run back, but Ivy's reaction to being a wolf hadn't been the best.

The walk back would take about twenty minutes with how far we had run. About halfway, I stopped and carried Sara. I didn't know why she felt the need to run after us, but it was too far and fast for her.

"Is she okay?" Ivy was walking only slightly behind me now. "Why hasn't she shifted back?"

"She's fine. She's not used to running so far. Her prosthetic is back at the house and walking with just one leg in a forest is not the easiest thing to do." Sara made an annoyed noise in her throat.

"She doesn't have something for her wolf?" Ivy

reached a tentative hand forward. "Is it okay if I pet her?"

"We rarely pet each other. It's an intimate gesture." I grinned, thinking about petting her sometime soon. "As for something to help her wolf... she refuses because it makes her look weak."

"Oh." She dropped her hand as she fell into step beside me. "Does that matter?"

"Yes. We have a hierarchy." I sighed and kept my eyes straight ahead. "It will be interesting to see where you fit in."

"And Cole is what? The resident asshole of the pack?" She laughed, and I wanted to put my arm around her and kiss her forehead. He was prickly at times, but he would also be the first to give his life to protect members of his pack.

Cole's back tensed, and he clenched his fists at his side. I was glad he was holding his alpha instincts in because the last thing we needed was for her to be more scared than she already was. All things considered, she was handling the news she was a wolf fairly well.

"Cole is the alpha. He is the most dominant member of the pack, just like his father was before he got up there in age and had to retire." Being alpha was a lot of work and stress. I would never want to be in charge of keeping the peace and ensuring our entire kind wasn't discovered.

"So, an asshole. Got it. What are you? A beta?"

Did I have to answer her? Telling her I was the omega was akin to getting kicked in the nuts. It had taken a long time to make the adjustment to being the pack's emotional support scratching post, but the alternative was unacceptable.

Sara was the true omega, and while most acknowledged me in the role, a few made their opinions known anytime we were in wolf form. It was one of the many reasons Sara hated being a wolf.

"He's the heart of the pack." Cole turned his head just enough so we could see the side of his face, but he wasn't looking back at Ivy. "Without him, we'd be a mess."

My face flamed, and I rubbed the back of my neck. "The pack would be fine."

My family house came into view, and I breathed a sigh of relief that the conversation would end. It wasn't that I was ashamed of my position in the pack, I just didn't want my mate to perceive me as weak before she even understood what my role was.

When we got to the back door, Ivy came to an abrupt stop and looked down at the hammer and then at my face. "Wait, didn't I hit you in the jaw with the hammer?"

I set Sara down next to her prosthetic and she shifted while laughing. "It was the funniest thing I've seen in a long time. I'm sad I didn't get it on video."

Ivy grabbed my arm as I went to walk in and turned me around. My eyes widened as she put her hand on my jaw and stroked it. "You wolves really need to work on your new wolf bedside manner. I'm sorry for whacking you with my hammer."

"I... uh... yeah." I was speechless as her warm hand

caressed my jaw. Did she know we were mates? "It's fine. My jaw. My jaw is fine."

"Oh, for fuck's sake." Sara stood. "Let's get you a robe or something."

"Clothes would be nice." Ivy took a blanket off the couch as soon as we were inside.

"Sara already put clothes back at my place for you. She is much smaller than you, so she got some from the other females until we can get your clothes." Cole was already waiting by the front door with his arms crossed over his chest.

Ivy grabbed the robe Sara brought out from her bedroom. "I'm going to pretend you didn't mean that like it sounded."

"What?" Cole could be dense sometimes.

"Sara is so much smaller than me." Her eyes twinkled as she teased him.

"I just meant..." He pinched the bridge of his nose. "Let's go."

She took the offered flip flops and followed Cole out of the house.

"I'll be home soon." I needed to talk to Sara about my feelings and what I should do with them.

After I shut the door, I turned back to a smirking Sara who threw a pair of shorts at me. "I've never seen either of you get so flustered over a girl."

"She's my mate, Sara." I pulled on my shorts. "My wolf is sure of it."

Her eyes widened, and she sat down heavily. "We don't have mates."

I headed to the liquor cabinet and pulled out a

bottle of whiskey. I wasn't a big drinker, but the realization that my feelings were an anomaly was a punch to the gut. She was different too, and not knowing anything about her put me on edge.

I took a swig and cringed as it burned going down. "I don't know what to do."

"Well, that's clear." Sara stood and snatched the bottle from me, putting it back in the cabinet. "If she really is your mate, you should act sooner rather than later. Cole had hearts in his eyes, and he never gets hearts in his eyes."

I rolled my eyes. "I don't think so. He's probably going to want to lock her in the basement again."

Sara snorted. "Men. You're so oblivious." She pulled me to the couch, and we sat down. "He was gentle with her, let her talk shit about him, and when she wasn't paying attention, he looked at her like he would move mountains for her."

"What am I supposed to do?" My experience with women was subpar. It wasn't that I'd purposely become an eternal bachelor, but no female wanted the one and only omega of the pack as a significant other. Even if I was attractive, smart, funny, and loving.

Which was exactly why I had dated a human for a few months on the downlow.

Sara got a dreamy look on her face. "What you do is woo her."

CHAPTER ELEVEN

Ivy

As we walked back to Cole's house, I couldn't help but look at his muscular ass and hamstrings. Holy cheese balls, I could bounce a quarter off those tight muscles. I'd always been a sucker for a man that took squats and deadlifts seriously.

His back was covered with a portrait of what I assumed was his wolf. It certainly looked like it. It was like he was watching me. It didn't escape my attention that he probably could have grabbed something to wrap around his waist, yet he hadn't. He wanted me to see his body.

Or it was like he said... they were used to being naked.

Why did the completely delicious ones have to be such jerks? It was a sick joke on poor women like me.

I needed to focus. Ogling the enemy was not a good idea. I had to learn about being a wolf as quickly as possible and then get the hell out of Dodge.

I already knew non-humans existed, but hadn't known wolves were part of the equation. When your best friend and her boyfriends jump in the water and their legs shift into tails, nothing is that surprising anymore.

But me being a wolf? I never thought I was anything but human. Is that why Riley and I had become instant best friends? Had we subconsciously sensed the otherness in each other?

There had to be a cure. I wasn't born this way, was I?

Cole slowed until I was walking next to him. His scent overwhelmed me and I held my breath for as long as I could. Everything smelled different and more... potent. Some things did *not* need to be smelled, that was for damn sure.

He stayed about two feet away, but his nearness still made my stomach swirl with something I didn't have a name for. I clenched my fists, and he rolled his eyes.

"You're different." As if I needed someone to tell me that.

"No shit. You think? I'm a wolf. Or having a hallucination from a brain injury. Maybe I'm in a coma?" I was rambling and talking to myself. If he hadn't thought I was crazy before, he might now.

I kept my eyes straight ahead, willing myself not to look at what he was packing in the front. It had been a while since I'd been with a man, and Cole was attractive. The urge to look was strong.

"The truck that made us crash. Who were they?" I hadn't pissed off any men recently, so they weren't after me.

"The other pack. They are also the same two that attacked the helicopter."

Well, that was just perfect. On top of worrying about myself turning into a wolf, now I had to worry about if other people would too... and then try to kill me.

Oh sweet wolves, was someone going to try to hump me and do that wolf knotting thing I'd read about?

The house came into view and I realized Cole wasn't just a volunteer helicopter pilot. Had he known all along I was a wolf and just gotten a job to scope me out? Did it even matter?

Now that I wasn't running for my life, I saw the house in all its glory. It was two stories with large windows and columns of stone and wood along the front. There was a porch that looked like it was perfect for drinking coffee and watching the world come alive in the morning.

The garage was in between the house and another building that was more industrial looking with roll up doors on the front. It was obscured by trees, but it was large.

Cole noticed where I was looking and lifted his chin in that direction. "That's where the pack meets and works out. They're going to want to meet you."

"Meet me?" I made a noise of disbelief. I was not about to walk into a building and meet a bunch of wolves. Wolves were wild animals, and sure I'd shifted into one, but I could stop it from happening again. Hopefully. "Are you under some delusion that I'm staying?"

He stopped just as we got to the steps leading onto the porch and turned to face me from two steps up. My eyes widened, and I looked to my left at a bush that was growing small buds.

He wasn't growing any small buds, that was for sure.

"I can take you to get some things from your house, but yes. You're staying here." He crossed his arms over his chest, and I looked back up at him. "Wolves can't live within the limits of Arbor Falls."

"I lived there for eight months and had no issues until *you* showed up! I'm not even a wolf. It was an optical illusion. I moonlight as a magician." I walked past him, bumping into him. "As soon as I get dressed, I'm going home."

"You are a new wolf that doesn't know how to control yourself. How do you plan on getting to your house? You've tried to leave twice now and look how far you got."

I was being a complete idiot and walking right back into the house where I had been locked in a cage. Right then, it seemed I had little choice. As soon as the time was right, I would escape and *not* get caught. Then I'd go straight to the hospital and have myself evaluated.

The tension I had felt gnawing at my insides lessened the second I stepped foot inside, despite my brain screaming to turn and run. My body had a different idea though, or maybe it was the other being lurking under the surface of my skin.

The entire living room and kitchen was decorated with warm shades of browns and creams, with stone lining one wall from floor to ceiling. The ceilings were high with dark wood beams, and a large light fixture made of wood that looked like antlers hung from the ceiling in the living room. One wall was all windows looking out at the forest.

Too bad there were cages in the basement.

"I have a room set up for you upstairs. Come on." My attention was ripped away from the beautiful view out the windows by Cole on the stairs.

"Uh, maybe I should go up first, so I don't have to look at all that." I waved my hand in his direction while looking away as I walked past him.

He chuckled. "You don't like the view? I could have sworn I felt your eyes searing into my ass cheeks on the walk back here."

I like the view too much, that's the problem.

I stopped at the top where there was a landing that split into two wings. In one direction were double doors, and in the other was a hallway with several rooms.

He took over the lead and stopped in front of an open room. I glanced inside and saw there was a small pile of clothes on the queen-sized bed. There was a dresser and desk all in matching white wood.

"There are towels and everything you might need in

the bathroom. When you're done, we'll talk more." He was giving me a look that I didn't know how to read. It almost looked wistful, but was so out of place on him, that I was probably imagining it.

An awkward moment passed before he turned and walked toward the set of double doors across the landing. I entered the room and locked the door behind me. It seemed pointless because I was sure he could kick it down with one swift kick of his heavily muscled leg.

I surveyed the room, appreciating the large window and the white bedding. It was clean and comfortable. I was tempted to just crawl into it, but I reeked.

The bathroom was cozy but had a large stall shower. I dropped the robe and braved a glance in the mirror. I fought back tears at my appearance. My skin was so caked with dirt and dried blood, I could barely even see skin. My hair looked like one big rat's nest, and I flinched at how much it was going to hurt to yank the tangles out of it.

On the counter was a brush, which I used before turning on the shower. I shouldn't have cared so much after going through hell, but a small piece of my remaining dignity had died when I looked in the mirror. They all had seen me like this.

I got most of the tangles out and then stepped into the shower. As the warmth hit my skin, I shut my eyes and let the water run over me for several minutes before I set to work trying to clean myself.

No amount of scrubbing cured the filth I felt inside. I'd killed a creature with my teeth and then ripped into its flesh. It was *not* the same as eating a juicy steak or a hamburger. You don't feel your food take its last breath.

Wrapping a soft towel around myself after drying off, I looked through the clothes left on the bed. There were a few pairs of leggings, oversized shirts, and new underwear. Hopefully, I'd be wearing my own clothes soon.

After getting dressed and tying the large shirt in a knot at the bottom, I went back to the bathroom to brush my teeth. I pulled back my lips, examining my teeth. They looked the same, maybe whiter than they used to be, but my vision was crisper now, so maybe they had always been that white.

My eyes looked brighter, like there had been a thin film covering them before, and now they shined with a gloss that seemed unnatural.

The thought of sinking my teeth into the poor deer flashed across my mind again, and I gripped the edge of the counter. It had tasted... good.

I felt a sharp pinch in my mouth and pulled back my lips again. "No, no, no!" I ran my tongue over sharp canines. I clutched my chest, feeling like my heart was going to explode. I couldn't breathe. Was it normal to pop canines while standing on two feet?

I got my shit together before rushing from the room and down the hall. I hesitated for a moment before raising my fist and pounding on the doors to Cole's room. No one answered, so I let myself in since it was unlocked.

The shower was running and music was coming from the bathroom. I never took Cole for a music in the shower type. Was he dancing and humming along to it?

I tried to calm myself and ended up sitting on the edge of the bed. I wouldn't barge into the bathroom. Although, he deserved to have his privacy and dignity ripped away from him. The door was half open, but I couldn't make out anything with the angle I was at.

It would have been the perfect time to escape, but I had no clue where keys to vehicles were kept or if I would attack someone if I shifted again. My pulse increased at the thought of attacking a person.

Holy fuck. What if I shifted while driving?

Needing to do something before I hyperventilated, I stood and went to the nightstand, biting my lip before opening it. I didn't know Cole that well, and people hid a lot of secrets in their nightstands.

A small box of condoms stared back at me, which made me grit my teeth. The copper taste of blood filled my mouth, and I cursed under my breath. Why did I care? I shouldn't have, but imagining Cole slipping one on and pounding some chick until she was boneless made me want to scream.

Next to them was a deadly-looking knife in a sheath, which I promptly took. He had to have a gun somewhere. No man brings a gun to work on his first day without more where that came from.

I checked under the pillows and ran my hand under the edges of the mattress. That was where people in movies kept them, wasn't it? This was right up there in fictional land.

I made it halfway down the other side of the bed

before my fingers brushed a gun handle. I pulled it out carefully. It was a pistol. That was about all I knew. My knowledge of weapons was courtesy of video games.

The shower turned off, which only spiked my heart rate further. I shoved the gun and knife in the waistband of my leggings, hoping I could keep them from falling. I untied the shirt and let it fall over the waistband. It was big enough to hide the bulge the weapons made.

I stood near the foot of the bed and locked my eyes on the bathroom mirror. When his wet body came into view, I stifled a satisfied sigh. What was wrong with me?

His eyes met mine in the bathroom mirror and he wrapped a towel around his waist before coming into the bedroom, water still running down his body. My eyes tracked a drop as it traveled down his muscular chest to the edge of the towel.

"What are you doing in here?" He looked from me to the open door and back again. "Did you knock?"

"You seriously did not just ask me that after keeping me locked *naked* in a basement. You're lucky I didn't come in there and cut off your-"

He waved his hand as if to dismiss my commentary. "What is it?"

I swallowed and ran my tongue over my teeth, which had thankfully returned to normal. "Are my teeth supposed to just... come out when I'm looking in the mirror?"

His eyes widened, and he ran his hand over his face

before running it back over his head. "Pups have that issue."

Pups? They called their babies pups? I didn't know whether to be horrified that they took being wolves so seriously or gush over how cute it was. "What about adults?"

"Ones that have lost their minds." He went to his dresser and pulled out a pair of black boxer briefs. "Were you thinking about the deer?"

He was not helping the situation at all. "Yes, but I feel incredibly guilty about killing it."

He slid his boxers on under his towel before throwing it onto the counter in the bathroom. "You'll get used to it. It will just take some time."

He slid into some jeans and I practically salivated at how they fit him perfectly with his V with a light trail of dark hair leading down into them. His body was a work of art with muscles that weren't too bulky but strong. His pecs were tattooed, and both arms had tattoo sleeves.

"How much time? I have work and a life. People are going to wonder where I am." I was glad I'd taken two days off work for my birthday. Too bad I spent those days locked up and passed out.

"I know you don't want to hear this, but it would be in your best interest to stay here. It's not safe in Arbor Falls, and I'd hate for the other pack to get a hold of you." He was talking to me as he went into his closet and then came back out, pulling on a gray shirt.

He looked amazing in gray, and I bit my lip. "And this pack is better than that one? Who says I want to be in a pack at all? Maybe shifting was just a two-time thing because of danger."

"Even more reason for you to be here. Your shifting is inconsistent. You should have complete control over the shift whether you're scared, angry, or just want to go for a run." He came closer, and I backed toward the door. "You aren't leaving, Ivy."

Before I could back out of the door, he trapped me against the door that wasn't open. There was something keeping me from kneeing him in the balls and darting out of the room.

"Why do you even care?" I whispered.

He brought his lips next to my ear. "You're my mate."

CHAPTER TWELVE

Ivy

"Come on, Ivy. Open the door." Cole had been outside my room for several minutes, trying to convince me to open the door. I was surprised he hadn't busted it down by now.

After he had told me I couldn't leave and I was his mate, I had run back to my temporary room and locked myself inside. I stashed the gun and knife under the mattress, not even sure why the hell I had taken them.

I paced in front of the window, considering my next move. Everything was happening so fast, and to make it worse, Cole Asshole Delaney said he was my mate. If being mates with a person meant you wanted to scream in frustration, then paranormal romance writers had gotten it all wrong. Wasn't I supposed to see hearts and want to rip his clothes off?

Ripping his clothes off appealed to me.

I put my palms against my eyes and groaned. I did not need to be thinking about him naked. What I needed was to figure out how to live with the fact that I was a cold-blooded Bambi killer.

The deer crossed my mind again, and tears welled in my eyes. I hated crying, but the tears wouldn't stop.

I pulled the covers back on the bed and buried myself in their warmth. I would just hide until I woke up from my nightmare. At least Cole went away, but he wasn't gone from my thoughts. I was drawn to him in a train wreck, moth to a flame, deer in the headlights kind of way.

Ugh, deer.

I must have fallen asleep for a while, because when I woke to knocking at my door, it was dark outside. I moaned and put a pillow over my head, hoping it would drown out the knocking and irritating voice on the other side.

"We're eating dinner if you want to join us." Cole ceased knocking, and I heard him retreat.

My stomach growled, and I groaned. I needed to eat real food to keep my energy up and my mind clear.

I quickly threw my hair in a bun and went downstairs. Cole and Eli were sitting at the kitchen table and looked up as I got to the bottom of the stairs. I half expected them to be eating in front of the television.

I walked across the room, trying not to stare too

hard at the man feast in front of me. It was hard, though. Really, really hard.

They were both attractive, but in completely different ways. Cole had a dangerous, don't fuck with me aura about him, while Eli looked like all he wanted to do was cuddle.

Eli was taller, slimmer, and younger than Cole, but he was still muscular. His skin was a soft brown tone that looked like he spent a lot of time in the sun, and his hair was jet black and short. He had the faintest hint of a five o'clock shadow. His dark brown eyes sparkled as they met mine.

The smell of meat hit my nose, and I growled lightly in my throat. *Down, girl.*

I plopped down at the circular table in between Cole and Eli and stared at the plate that was set for me. I inhaled deeply and could smell each individual ingredient as it entered my nose.

The venison was cooked rare with a fragrant blackberry reduction. It smelled so good I didn't hesitate to grab my fork and knife, even though in the back of my mind I wondered if it was the deer I had killed that morning.

As I took the first bite, I couldn't stop the small moan from escaping. Both men stared at me with heated eyes.

"Why are you staring?" I knew exactly why they were staring. If they were going to hold me against my will, I would not make it easy on them.

Cole started eating his own dinner, and Eli took a

sip of his wine but didn't touch his plate. The silence was killing me, mainly because I had so many questions. The most important question being who the cook was because I needed to get on their good side.

I sighed as I finished the last bite and sat back in my chair. I was glad my body wanted cooked food.

"Do you want more?" Eli gestured to the food on his plate.

Was that why he waited until I was done? I wasn't an expert on wolves, but that was something an omega did; wait until the pack was done eating. Only, I wasn't part of their pack and we weren't sporting tails at the moment.

"I'm good. It was delicious though." I blotted my lips with my napkin and Eli finally started eating. I stayed focused on him, since he wasn't the one proclaiming I was his mate. "My friends and work are going to be worried when I don't show up on Monday."

Cole took a drink of what looked like whiskey and cleared his throat. "Eli sent an email from your phone requesting a leave of absence for personal reasons. Is there anyone else we need to contact?"

"My phone is still in one piece? I want it back." I looked at Eli, who had his eyes focused on his plate. "Eli, help me out here."

"Can't do that." He cringed and looked up at me through his long eyelashes. Damn, the whole bashful thing from him was cute as hell.

"It's too risky." Cole refilled my wine glass, which got a look of annoyance from Eli.

I stared at him as if he had ten heads and a monkey tail. "Too risky? We're talking about upheaving my entire life! How is letting me talk to people I know a risk? I'm not going to tell them." Except Riley. Maybe.

I snatched the wine glass and gulped it down. I should have just taken the entire bottle from him and chugged it.

"We'll text people on your behalf. We thought that you could say you're going to a wellness retreat or rehab for a drinking problem." Cole shrugged as if it was no big deal. "It would have been too suspicious for both of us to quit at the same time. Even though I was volunteering my time, I told Barbara I would stay until she found a new pilot."

"A drinking problem?" I grabbed the wine bottle and took a drink from it because I couldn't resist. "You never answered my question."

"I don't trust that you won't expose us." Cole took the wine bottle from me and set it down. "We know nothing about you."

Unbelievable. My patience had worn out, and I grabbed my steak knife, standing with it in my hand. I didn't quite know what my aim was, but the voice in my head, which I had determined was my wolf, was egging me on. I wasn't going to stab him with it.

Cole stood abruptly and stared me down, his eyes blazing. "Try it." The challenge hung in the air for several long moments before Eli reached over and pried my hand from the knife.

"Now, now, children. Let's try to get along. Maybe a

violent video game will help." He laughed uneasily and put the knife on the other side of his plate.

"Sit down," Cole warned, his eyes still locked on mine. He was back to his bossy, infuriating self.

"No." I folded my arms across my chest. Who the hell did he think he was, bossing me around like I was a child?

"Why is she not-" Eli was cut off by Cole.

"Shut up," he bit out, throwing his napkin that was clutched in his fist on his plate. He took his drink and hastily walked down the hallway where the door to the basement was. I heard a door slam and flinched.

I sat back down with a huff, grabbed the bottle of wine, and took another chug. "What crawled up his ass and died?"

Eli tilted his head slightly to the side as if his wolf was in control, his eyes flashing amber for a moment, like it had come to the surface. "Cole is the alpha and you're in his territory. You shouldn't be challenging him like you are, even in human form. If he says to sit, you sit."

I snorted in disbelief. The wolf thing, yeah, okay, I was a wolf, and they were wolves. But a pack mentality? I wasn't sure I could handle taking orders or being a submissive... bitch. "You thought *that* was me challenging him? I'm just getting started."

"You're playing with fire then." Eli stood and started clearing the dishes.

"Maybe I like to feel the burn," I muttered, cradling the wine bottle to my chest. It was some vintage red that probably cost an arm and a leg, and I planned on drinking all of it.

He hummed as he rinsed the plates he had set in the sink. "I think what we need is a movie night. Unless you're tired."

"I'm not tired. I took a pretty long nap." I stood up to help him clear the table. "Do you live here too?"

"Yes. I have a suite down here. Cole's my best friend, and I make sure he's taken care of. The pack hangs out here a lot too, mostly out back or in the den and gym next door. Cole told them to stay away until we made sure you weren't rabid."

"Gee, thanks." I handed him the rest of the dishes from the table.

"By the way, Cole hates when dishes are in the sink. Shall we watch a movie?" Eli left all the dishes in the sink and walked out of the kitchen with a smirk on his face.

I was glad to see he liked to poke the bear. Watching Cole lose his shit made me giddy. I was twenty-six, but that didn't mean I had to act like it all the time.

Eli sat down on the large sectional that looked like it could easily fit ten people and turned on the flat screen above the fireplace. I sat a safe distance away from him, put the bottle of wine on the coffee table, and hugged a pillow to my chest.

I was conflicted. On one hand, I knew I needed to be there with them. On the other, I just wanted to go back to my life and pretend nothing was real. But it was real. I wasn't in denial. As a teenager, I had seen for myself that there was another world right under the ocean. It only made sense there would be another world on land.

My mind never really focused on the romantic comedy movie Eli put on. Between going over my options and trying to figure out where they might have my phone, I was distracted. About an hour in, I felt like the world was pressing down on my chest.

"Is there a bathroom down here I can use?" I stood and stretched.

"Third door on the left. Do you want me to pause?" He hadn't looked away from the screen. He was more into the romantic comedy than I'd thought.

"No. I've seen it." I hadn't, but it didn't matter since I'd already missed half of it.

I made my way down the hall, passing the busted door to the basement and trying to remember if Eli had said the third door on the right or third door on the left.

I opened the door next to the basement, and instead of a bathroom, the garage greeted me. I had lived in a pretty big house growing up, but it had nothing on this house. It probably could have fit even more vehicles than it had if he moved them forward and parked them bumper to bumper.

It was an impressive collection. I had never imagined garages this size existed outside of mega mansions. There was an oversized SUV, a motorcycle, two fancy cars, and enough off-road vehicles for half a dozen people. Plus, there was the truck with the crashed car in the driveway.

Cole had to be a drug dealer to afford all these

things. I didn't know much about sports cars, but they had to be expensive. Some had to belong to Eli.

I stepped into the garage, gently shutting the door behind me so I wouldn't draw attention to myself. I had thought I was going to be able to deal with my predicament, but reality really sank in as I had tried to relax in the living room. I had been so tense that when I finally let go even just a little, my mind caught up.

I needed to sleep in my bed and wear my own clothes. Maybe I wasn't as accepting of the situation as I told myself I was.

I tentatively approached the cars and peered inside them. I don't know what I had hoped to find. Nothing would have changed from when I had looked in the morning, but I had a small sliver of hope that maybe I'd get lucky.

Not finding any keys, my last bit of courage left me in a rush, and I let out a cry of frustration. I sat down on the hard cement and leaned against a car, bringing my knees to my chest. I buried my face in my arms and let myself have a moment of weakness.

I cried for what felt like a lifetime before sensing eyes on me. I lifted my head to find Cole leaning with his hip against a car, arms crossed. He was the last person I wanted to see. Now he knew I was a weak, blubbering mess.

"Why are you out here?" His eyes flashed with concern, but it was gone in an instant.

"Why are *you* out here?" I spat back. I picked myself up off the floor and held my head up high despite the red puffiness I knew always plagued my face after crying.

"It's *my* garage." He pushed off the car with his hip and stood blocking my path back to the door as I went to walk past him.

He smelled like whiskey and carnauba wax, making the wolf part of me want to whimper in glee. She liked him a little too much for my taste. It was an odd feeling, having something inside me that had its own set of feelings and thoughts.

"Well, since it's yours, I guess I should leave." I tried to scoot past him, but he moved to block me. "Let me go, Cole."

I wasn't above fighting my way past him if I had to. His frequent shows of dominance were pissing me and my wolf off.

"We need to talk." Of course, he wanted to talk about things I didn't want to talk about at the worst possible time.

"Maybe tomorrow." I pushed past him.

He wrapped his arm around my waist and spun me around. My canines snapped out of hiding, and I growled as he pulled me against his chest, one of his hands on the back of my head.

What on Earth was he doing?

He pulled the ponytail holder out of my hair and buried his face in it, his chest rumbling against my cheek. "Mine."

Taking deep breaths, I tried to calm myself and not to react, but the smell of his shirt made me rub my cheek against his chest.

I wanted him.

I pulled away and ran back into the house. I found the bathroom and locked myself inside. I was in way over my head.

CHAPTER THIRTEEN

Ivy

The walls were closing in on me, and I needed to get out of the house. Despite waiting it out in the bathroom, my teeth refused to go away. I still heard the movie playing down the hall, and I hadn't heard Cole come in from the garage.

My wolf was starving even though I had just eaten. Was that normal? She had just mauled a deer twelve hours ago, and I had a hearty dinner, and now she wanted more?

I eyed the bathroom window and then looked down at my bare feet. They were giving me my space; it was the perfect opportunity to make a run for it.

I flipped the latch on the window and pushed it up. My wolf, who was waiting impatiently, yipped in agreement. It was weird being able to sense something else inside of me and hear her like she was right by my side.

She didn't want to escape, though. She wanted Cole. She wanted Eli. She wanted all the deer. The thought of deer had a low growl rising in my throat. Maybe after a quick snack, she'd calm down.

Oh my God, what am I even thinking?

I popped off the screen and let it fall to the ground outside. I had never snuck out of a window before, and it was awkward standing on the toilet and trying to get my body out of the window without falling on my head. Everyone in college always talked about sneaking out of their bedroom windows when they were younger, like it was no big deal. I felt like a contortionist.

I managed not to break my neck as I landed on the hard ground and quickly took off my clothes, laying them on the windowsill. I could run faster as a wolf. My wolf sat and cocked her head to the side, but I stayed human. It wasn't even that I could visualize her, I just *knew* that was what she was doing.

How did this even work? After several frustrating minutes of huffing and puffing, trying to shift to my wolf, I pulled my clothes back on and ran toward the trees.

I sniffed the air and followed a promising scent. It was strange to be sniffing the air for an animal to kill, but my wolf's need was engulfing my brain. Yet, she sat and waited.

I came to a stop and inhaled deeply. A smorgasbord of deer was just ahead.

I peeked out from behind a tree and spotted two deer standing near each other. They were resting but had their eyes open. My wolf took over, and I attacked so fast that neither deer had time to react before I tackled the larger one, shifting as my body hit it.

My mind went blank as I tore into it. I could have tried to stop myself, but then what? I'd attack another animal later?

After finishing, I let out a satisfied burp, and with little thought, shifted back and stood. I looked away as I backed up from the gruesome scene in front of me. My canines were no longer out, but it left me with a feeling of disgust.

I dropped to my knees with tears streaming down my face. "I'm so, so sorry." I knew it couldn't hear me—because it was dead—but it made me feel a little better, although not much.

My wolf was uncontrollable.

Fuck. I couldn't just go back home. What if I shifted and killed someone because there were no deer nearby? I was there now, and the other option was to go home and wolf out without meaning to. As much as I hated admitting it, I needed to stay, at least for a bit.

I hated feeling like I was helpless, and I hated that I didn't even know how I'd come to be. Had someone in Cole's pack or the other pack abandoned me? Why would they do that? Was there something wrong with me?

Admitting to myself that I was going to have to rely on Cole to help me was a tough pill to swallow. I didn't want to give in so easily, but the dead deer lying ten feet away told me differently.

I stood and wiped the dirt off my knees. It was the second time in one day I'd have to do the naked walk of shame back to the house. I didn't know what wolf etiquette was, but I didn't have the tools to bury the deer.

I wrapped my arms around my middle as I walked, trying to keep myself warm. I could barely see the lights from the house when I heard growls behind me. *Now what?*

Turning, I covered myself the best I could and faced two wolves who were not the three I knew. They snarled at me and lowered themselves as if they were going to stalk forward.

I felt the smallest jolt and was falling before I processed I was shifting. My legs caught me, and I snarled back at the wolves who had moved toward me as if stalking their prey. The last thing I wanted was a wolf fight, but I was excited and yearning to put these two in their place. They were disrespecting me by showing me their teeth.

I turned my attention to the larger male and growled, showing my own teeth. My tail stood straight up and the hair on my hackles bristled. I crouched and lunged forward at the same time he did.

We clashed, snarling and biting into each other. The other wolf backed out of the way and cowered as he watched the fight. We rolled around on the ground before separating and continuing to circle each other.

He had bitten my hind leg, which was dripping blood, but I could already feel it healing.

"Enough. He is pack." The voice entered my head, and I snapped my attention to the approaching gray wolf with a snarl.

Cole. Alpha. Mate. Mine.

I snapped at him and lowered my body in a crouch, ready to spring if he rubbed me the wrong way. Maybe I needed to be locked back up after all.

"Don't test me Ivy, I don't want to fight you."

Before I could stop my wolf, I jumped and butted my head into his side, sending him flying. He grunted but was up quickly and was pissed.

"I warned you." He charged, and we tumbled across the ground.

He quickly pinned me under his much larger wolf and snarled in my face. My heart clenched, and I shrank back from him but refused to look away. My wolf really wanted to look down, but I didn't let her.

"I'm the alpha of this pack and you need to learn to show some respect." His voice was a snarl in my head. *"The first thing you're going to do is apologize to Manny and Dante. Then you and I are going to go back to the house and lay down some ground rules."*

He had to be kidding. *"They are the ones that came at me growling. I was protecting myself!"* Well, mostly.

"You were challenging one of my betas!" His voice was a roar and made me flinch under his strong paws, the nails slightly digging into my shoulders. *"And then you challenged* me *in front of them. Do you have any idea what I usually do to wolves who challenge me?"*

It was unnerving getting a lecture from a wolf inside my head.

"Make sweet wolf love to them?" I caught him off guard with my retort and he shifted his weight. I rolled out from under him before he could recover. *"I win, wolf boy. Catch me if you can."*

I let out several celebratory and slightly deranged yips before taking off at full speed toward the house. My wolf and I were going to get along just fine. It seemed like the more we acknowledged each other's existence, the more in sync we were.

I heard him behind me, and I wasn't sure what he was going to do to me for that little show, but it made a rush of excitement flood my system. I tumbled forward, shifting back to human. There had to be a secret to doing it on command because I sucked at it.

I face planted in some leaves and groaned, turning my head to spit out a leaf. Bare feet came to a stop in front of me, and I reached out and patted the top of his foot.

"Please say my punishment is a spanking." I glanced up at him, his face barely visible in the moonlight. I could see his eyes though, and they burned a hole right through me.

He reached down and yanked me up by my arm before releasing me and taking off toward the house. He was livid, but his eyes had also burned with desire.

I ran after him, concerned with his quietness. A part of me was excited every time we exchanged words. My wolf was not happy he was walking away.

"I was hungry." My skin prickled as I followed him

into the warm house, hoping my vague explanation was enough to warrant a response. It didn't, and he made his way toward the stairs. "Say something, Cole."

The living room was empty and most of the house dark. Eli was nowhere to be seen or heard, which left us alone.

A small spark of something unexpected made its way through my body as I followed Cole's nakedness up the stairs. I wanted him in a deep, soul-crushing kind of way.

My wolf whimpered as he shut his bedroom door without a look back in my direction.

~

I STARED AT THE CEILING, replaying the events of the day. I should have wanted to sleep, but my mind wouldn't quiet down. A tight knot had formed in my stomach at the realization I was inexplicably drawn to Cole. The more I was around him, the worse it became.

Maybe he really was my mate.

Before I chickened out, I got out of bed and went down the hall to his door. It was just past three in the morning, and instead of sleeping, all I could think about was *him*.

I knocked lightly on his door and got no response, but that was expected since he was sleeping. Biting my lower lip, I took a breath and opened the door, slipping inside. I didn't know what I was doing, but the pull to be close to him was strong.

He was spread out on top of his covers, face down.

He stirred as I made my way into his room but didn't wake. He was much less intimidating sprawled out in only his boxer briefs. I appreciated how they formed tightly around his butt.

"Cole?" He grumbled and rolled onto his side. I took a few more steps toward the bed.

I lowered myself next to him, staring at his face. He looked so peaceful that I regretted coming in and disturbing him. He was probably still pissed at me and would probably kill me for waking him up.

Unable to help myself, I reached out my hand and cupped his stubbled cheek. His eyes cracked open, and he stared back at me with sleepy brown eyes.

"It's not wise to sneak into a wolf's den in the middle of the night." His voice was soft and raspy. "Did you come to apologize?"

He had to ruin the moment. I looked down at his lips and then back up at his eyes. My breath caught in my throat as his hand snaked around my back and pulled me to him.

"Because if you're here in my bed to apologize..." He had pulled me all the way against him and had his lips against my ear. Sweet baby fawn, this was not what I was expecting. Maybe he was still asleep. "Start apologizing."

His lips touched right below my ear, and a moan escaped before I could help myself. He continued trailing his lips down my neck, causing my breath to hitch. Our legs had somehow become entwined, and I felt the urge to move my body against his. His lips reached the neck of my shirt and he lightly nipped at my skin with his teeth.

"Cole." My voice sounded like some sex-crazed vixen. He continued trailing his lips along my skin, and his hand slid under my shirt. "Cole." I said it more firmly.

"Hm?" His lips were on my jaw and inching closer to my mouth, his hand already halfway up my stomach.

"You said we needed to lay some ground rules," I breathed.

His fingers brushed right under my breast. He was way too good at driving me crazy. His lips slid over mine before I could speak again, making me completely forget about rules.

I completely forgot everything. What was my name? The world fell away, and it was just the two of us, connecting for the first time.

He brought his other hand behind my head and deepened the kiss. My hands made their way to the edge of his boxers and he moaned against my lips.

My brain had just wrapped around the fact that I was making out with Cole of all people when he pulled his lips away from mine. His jaw ticked and his eyes flashed amber, his wolf peeking through. "I accept your apology. Now get out of my room."

My stomach dropped, and I brought a hand up to touch his face, but he moved his head to avoid it. "What?" I muttered, confusion in my voice. "You... we..."

"Never challenge me again." He turned over with his back facing me. "Goodnight, Ivy."

I got up and made my way to the door before I lost

it in front of him. My wolf was more upset at the rejection than I was, but if she was upset, then so was I.

"I thought I was your mate." I opened the door, but before walking out I stopped. I mustered up all the strength I could to keep my voice from shaking. "You will never be my mate or my alpha."

I slammed the door and choked back my sob as I made my way back to my bedroom.

CHAPTER FOURTEEN

Cole

Fuck.

I rolled onto my back after the door slammed and stared at the ceiling. Why wasn't there an instruction manual for women? Her final words before leaving had stung, but I had deserved them.

I shouldn't have kissed her, and I definitely shouldn't have turned my back on her. My wolf had been beside himself. His mate, yet his adversary. What a clusterfuck.

I rubbed a hand over my face and sat up. There was no way I was going to sleep after touching her like I did and then hurting her.

I threw on a pair of sweatpants and opened my door. I didn't know what the hell I was doing, but the guilt swirling inside me was making me feel sick.

Alphas didn't feel guilty for disciplining their pack when they got out of line. Was she even pack?

She had to be *something* because I could talk to her through my alpha connection. She might have accepted being part of the pack without even realizing she'd done so.

I walked to the guest bedroom, put my ear against the door, and shut my eyes. I heard sniffles, and my chest seized knowing I'd caused it.

I knocked and then opened the door. She had her back to me, and a deep longing filled my chest. Was this what it was supposed to feel like to have a mate?

I shut the door behind me and sighed. "Look, I'm a dick." She snorted a tear-filled laugh. "I don't know how to do this. This whole thing is uncharted territory for me, and I'm sorry."

She sat up and turned to face me, wiping her cheeks. She had fire in her eyes, and I leaned back against the door, ready to take the tongue lashing she was about to give me.

"You can't just expect me to know all the wolf and pack rules. I didn't know what the fuck I was doing out there. They growled at me, and I defended myself the best way I knew how, by fighting. Maybe instead of being mad at me, you should be mad at the male members of your pack for approaching a female that's much smaller who was naked and alone." She scooted to the edge of the bed and crossed her arms over her chest. "And then you scolded me like I was a child. I don't like being bossed around by men. I swore when I was eighteen that I'd never let another man take advantage of me again."

"Did someone hurt you?" If someone had hurt her, I'd find them and kill them.

She bit her lip. "He's been dealt with. That's not the point. I won't be in a pack that uses wolf hierarchy to mistreat others."

I pushed off the door and sat next to her on the bed, leaving enough space between us so she wouldn't be uncomfortable. "Our wolves have a mind of their own."

"That's a bullshit excuse. I've only known my wolf for a day, and I already know I will eventually be the boss."

I fought a smile. "You're a little firecracker, aren't you?"

"Only when I need to be." She crawled back under the covers. "What now?"

I stood and looked down at her. Her red hair fanned across the pillow, and I was tempted to lie down next to her and run my fingers through it. That ship probably had sailed.

"You learn to be a wolf."

∼

I LOOKED over to check on Ivy as we drove down the gravel road toward the highway. Her hand was resting on her cheek as she watched the scenery out the passenger side window.

After repeatedly apologizing the night before, there

had been a few moments of awkwardness before I'd patted her head and went back to my room. Who the hell pats an attractive woman's head? This idiot, that's who.

I slowed the truck as we came to some of the pack's teenagers playing catch in the middle of the road.

"How many of you are there?" Ivy didn't look at me, but at least she was talking.

She had been quiet at breakfast and had shown little excitement when I announced we'd be going to her house to pick up things she needed. I thought she would have been happy at my olive branch.

"Three hundred and twenty-six, including you." We were one of the smaller packs since conflict split us. Some chose sides and some left to live with other, less drama-filled packs.

I couldn't blame them. If I would have had the choice, I would have left too.

"How do you not end up marrying your cousins?" She didn't sound like she was joking.

A laugh burst out of me as I came to a stop at the end of the road. I waited until I turned onto the highway to answer. "Pack members move around to different packs when they're younger to go to college or to be closer to a job that's wolf shifter friendly. Plus, there's a dating app called Hounder."

She clutched the door handle. "You're kidding, right?"

"No." I briefly glanced over at her white knuckling the door. "Are you okay?"

"The last time you were at the wheel, we crashed." She took a few deep breaths and her grip loosened.

"What if someone in your pack falls in love with the enemy pack?"

I grumbled under my breath, and she finally turned her head to look at me with raised eyebrows. She probably didn't want to hear about pack politics. Hell, even I got sick of the bullshit.

"I don't want to bore you." Pack relations was a topic that drove me up a wall. It wasn't that difficult to get along with others, even if you didn't like them. What made it difficult was when one party held some ill-conceived belief that the other had wronged them.

"It won't bore me. They tried to kill us, didn't they? I should know why." She had a point.

"We used to be one pack under one alpha. My father and Silas's father were the alpha's betas. When we were both around eight, the alpha was murdered, and they accused each other of killing him." I shook my head, remembering the war that started between my father and Silas's. "They maintained that my father had done it so he could be the alpha of the pack."

"And where are both of your fathers now?" she asked carefully. I could see where her mind went.

"Retired. As we get older, our wolves get weaker and the alpha position usually passes to a son who is in a beta position. The strongest in the pack is the one that has the most connection to all the other wolves in the pack."

"What if the alpha doesn't have a son?" I groaned at her question because I was certain she'd have her opinions on how things were.

"Even if I were to have only a daughter, she can't be

the alpha. Female wolves can be strong, but not enough to lead a pack. So, it passes to the beta or the beta's son."

"Of course that's how it is," she scoffed.

I needed to choose my words carefully. "It's the wolf part, not the human part. A female head of pack? Sure there is the lead female who is stronger than all the other females, but there might be dozens of men stronger than her in wolf form. It's nature."

"Well, nature sucks." She looked back out the window. "What about my parents? My coloring is different than all the wolves I've seen so far."

"Yeah." I reached forward to turn on the radio. "There aren't red wolves."

"So, I'm a freak?" She crossed her arms over her chest. "Great."

"That's not what I said." *River* by Leon Bridges played in the background. "Just because your hair is a different color than the rest of us doesn't make you any less of a wolf. Once we get you settled, we'll work on figuring out your origin."

"Get off."

"What?" It took me a moment to realize she meant *get off the highway*, and I chuckled under my breath. I might have almost been thirty-five, but I would always chuckle at a sexual innuendo, whether it happened on purpose or accident.

"You missed that opportunity last night, unfortunately." There was a hint of teasing in her voice and pink crept onto her cheek.

I took the exit for Main Street and the rest of the

way to her house was silent besides the radio and her giving me the occasional direction.

I backed into the driveway of her house, which was not what I was expecting. I had expected an apartment or possibly a duplex. Instead, she lived in a craftsman style house with a well-maintained lawn.

"You live here alone?" I turned off the truck, and we got out. I grabbed the boxes and tape I'd brought from the back.

"Yes, I bought it as soon as I moved here permanently." She walked up the front steps onto the porch and unlocked the door. We had luckily found her purse still intact in the wreckage of my car and salvaged her keys, wallet, and phone.

I followed her inside and inhaled. Her scent was so strong I had to swallow my groan. My dick twitched in my jeans, and I moved the boxes so she wouldn't see my growing erection.

The interior was remodeled but still had all the elements I would expect in a craftsman with exposed wood beams, built-in cabinetry, tapered posts, and window castings. My wolf whined just under the surface as we took in our mate's den.

"This is pretty impressive for being twenty-six." I followed her up the stairs, trying not to breathe in any more of her scent or look at the way her ass moved in the leggings she had on.

Her smell was overwhelming me in a way I'd never experienced before. I'd had my fair share of partners, but none of them ever elicited this kind of visceral reaction from me or my wolf. Was she feeling the same way, or did she feel nothing?

"You can just wait in the living room. I need to clean out the refrigerator of anything that's going to spoil if you want to help." She stopped at her bedroom door and turned to face me. "What's wrong? You look… pained."

She took the boxes and tape from me, and our fingers brushed, sending a jolt of desire straight up my arm, through my heart, then right down to my cock. Her hand lingered for a minute before she turned and walked into her bedroom.

"Just wolf stuff." I followed her in and looked around the space. It was a typical bedroom, but it was so much more than that. It was where she laid her head every night and probably brought men up to. I tamped down on a growl.

The unmade bed had enough pillows to accidentally suffocate someone. The chair in the corner had a book on the cushion and an empty wine glass on the small table next to it. And the smell… I shut my eyes and inhaled.

"Did you just smell my room?" She sounded amused and taped the bottom of a box shut. "That's weird."

"You can tell a lot by what you smell. You should try it." I wasn't sure what to do to help, so I went to the chair and picked up the book, looking at the back. "Reverse harem?"

"Yes." She snatched it from me and threw it in the box. "There's nothing quite like a woman bringing multiple men to their knees."

I snorted and sat down, watching as she dumped her underwear and socks into the box. I felt useless, but it was better if I didn't touch her stuff.

"What did your nose tell you?" She opened her closet, and her scent hit me again.

I shifted in the chair and then widened my legs and leaned forward with my forearms on my knees. That should cover up what was happening to me. "That you haven't had a man in this room."

She plopped a suitcase on her bed and opened it. "Actually, there have been men in here."

"Not for sex."

"You got me there." She walked back in her closet and came back out with an armful of clothes on hangers, which she put in the suitcase. "What else?"

"You have nightmares."

"You can tell that from just sniffing the air? Shit, don't smell my bed." She laughed uncomfortably.

I didn't need to smell her bed. "I guess I should go start on the refrigerator so you can get anything you might need from your nightstand."

I left her room as she stared after me with her mouth wide open.

CHAPTER FIFTEEN

Ivy

I didn't know whether to be horrified or intrigued that he had mentioned my nightstand. As soon as I heard him walking down the stairs, I inhaled deeply to see what the hell he was talking about. I hadn't wanted to do it in front of him to give him the satisfaction of knowing I was eager to learn.

The first scent, and really the only scent that mattered to my wolf, was Cole. It was a warm scent, almost like cinnamon, and made me want to curl up in a ball and smell it all day. It also made a zing of lust shoot down my spine and settle in my gut.

I quickly finished packing some clothes, shoes, and toiletries and moved the boxes and suitcase outside the bedroom door. I couldn't get the scent of Cole out of my head. Sure, I'd been around him for the last day and even been in his bed, but inhaling deep did something to my insides.

I carried my suitcase downstairs, leaving it at the bottom, and walked into the kitchen to find Cole with the refrigerator door open.

"You don't have much in here to throw out. I put some stuff in your freezer." He shut the door and turned to look at me. "Are you all done packing?"

I stepped toward him and he backed up into the refrigerator as I crowded into his space. "Yes." My hands touched his waist, and I buried my face in his neck, inhaling.

He was the perfect height for nuzzling into his neck. A height where I'd just have to tip my chin in the slightest to meet his lips.

"Ivy," he warned in a gravelly voice that promised if I didn't back away from him, I was going to end up under him. "We should probably get going."

"When you came into my room last night to grovel, why didn't you kiss me again?" I nuzzled his neck and my entire body felt attuned to him.

One of his hands trailed lightly up and down my spine while the other moved my hair off my neck. His fingertips brushed the sensitive skin below my ear, and I hummed my approval.

"I figured you were pissed off still, and I didn't want to push my luck." He walked me backward until my ass hit the counter. "But I can't stop thinking about the taste of your lips or the feel of your skin."

I groaned as his lips brushed across the shell of my ear. "This is a bad idea." It might have been a bad idea, but it felt so good and right that I wasn't going to stop him.

Our lips met in a kiss that spoke more than we ever could. I wanted to dislike Cole, but my body had a different idea. My body was screaming at me not to stop.

He lifted me onto the counter, putting us at the same height, and I spread my legs for him to step closer. I *needed* him closer. If he pulled away from me, I would chase him down.

My fingers dug into his hair as our tongues met to explore each other's mouths. I wrapped my legs around him, my borrowed pair of flip-flops falling to the floor as I dug my heels into the muscular globes of his ass.

His scruff scratched against my neck as he kissed down my jawline. "Cole, you aren't going to stop, are you?" God, I sounded desperate. Maybe I was, but I didn't care.

"No." He sucked on my neck, marking me as he took hold of the hem of my shirt. "You don't want me to stop, do you?"

I shook my head, not trusting my voice to come out normal. A grin spread across his face as he pulled away and lifted my top over my head and threw it behind him. He stared down at my naked breasts and then grabbed a handful of my hair.

"Tell me you're mine." His lips trailed across my collarbone and down between my breasts. I scooted forward on the counter, trying to get closer to him. When I didn't respond, his lips stopped moving just as he was closing in on my nipple. "Tell me, Ivy."

"I can't." My chest was heaving, and I wondered if he was going to stop. I wasn't going to say something just because he told me to.

"Then I guess I'll just have to make you mine." His mouth latched onto my nipple and he bit, sending a sting of pain and a pang of pleasure between my legs.

I gripped his shoulders and moved my hips against him as he sucked and nipped at my nipples. I was all for foreplay, but the wetness between my legs and the burn that was starting to build was driving me crazy.

"I need you inside me, now." I pushed him back and leaned forward, reaching for the hem of his shirt.

He made a rumbling noise that was much more animalistic than I was used to and reached behind his neck, yanking his shirt off. "Take off your pants."

I slid off the counter and shimmied out of the yoga pants I was wearing. "You're a little bossy."

He kicked off his shoes and took off his pants. The kitchen seemed like the last place we should have sex, but before I could say anything, he lifted me back on the counter and took my mouth again.

I pulled away as he lined up with my entrance. "Wait, I don't know where you've been."

He gave me a funny look and then his face softened. "We don't get STIs."

"Well, that's reassuring, but what about getting pregnant? Does human birth control even work? I'm on it." I felt like I was ruining the moment, but the last thing I wanted when dealing with turning into a wild animal was carrying a baby too. "You had condoms in your nightstand."

Nice one, Ivy. Now he was going to know I took his knife and then assume I'd taken the gun too.

"How do you... never mind. Yes, it works, but you can only get pregnant during the full moon anyway." He cringed, probably from my expression. "I know, I know. Not exactly sexy talk."

I wrapped my arms around his neck. "Well then, tell me something sexy."

He put his lips by my ear as he grabbed his cock and rubbed it against my clit. "This morning in the shower, I got off thinking about burying my cock deep inside you."

He lined up with my entrance and slid in tantalizingly slow. I wrapped my legs around his waist. "More."

"I imagined how hot and wet you'd be for me and how your pussy would clench around me as I slid in and out." He began moving his hips in rolling motions that made my toes curl.

"And is it as you imagined?" I dug my nails into his shoulders as my head fell back.

He kissed along my neck. "It's tight and hot. Fuck, Ivy. It's like your pussy was made for me."

"Then fuck me." I was practically begging for him. His dick stretched me in a way that made my legs tremble, and I didn't want him to hold back.

He picked up the pace, the sound of our skin slapping together and the gasps and moans echoing in the kitchen.

Warmth spread across my entire body, and with every thrust, my clit throbbed, aching for relief of the pressure.

"I'm going to come," I panted against his mouth like some kind of animal.

He picked me up, turned, and walked to the kitchen table. I whimpered, not liking the sudden decrease in pace the move made. My ass hit the table and then he pulled out, leaving me feeling empty and wanting. I didn't have to wonder for long what he was doing because he pulled me up, spun me around, and pushed me down against the table so my ass was facing him.

"Cole. What are you-" His hand landed on my ass, and I yelped at the sting of pain as my pussy clenched around nothing.

"This ass is mine." He ran his hand over the burning globe as he kissed down my spine.

His teeth nipped at the skin where he had smacked before he kissed it. I held onto the side of the table and tried not to lose my mind.

"This crack is mine." He slid his hand down my crack as he kissed down to the backs of my thighs. "These legs are mine."

I was trembling as his hand cupped my pussy that was dripping with desire. I knew he was about to claim it, and I pushed my ass back and spread my legs.

"What else is yours?" My voice trembled as I waited for him to relieve the pressure between my legs.

His finger dipped between my folds and circled my clit. "This clit is mine."

"Oh, God, yes." I rested my cheek against the cool surface of the table. "Take it. Take it all."

"This pussy..." His finger circled my entrance. "Mm, most definitely mine."

"Please." I was going to combust.

"Please, what?" He slid a finger in, and I gripped the table.

"Fuck me, Cole. Fuck me into this table, just... make me yours." The words felt right, and I turned my head to look down at him. "Now."

He had the most serious expression of concentration on his face as he slid in a second finger. "Telling the alpha what to do?"

I gasped as he leaned forward and licked me from ass to clit, burying his face as he worked his tongue over my sensitive bud. My legs trembled as my orgasm built from the tips of my extremities.

"Yes!" I cried out as my orgasm barreled down my spine, and Cole continued to eat me like a feast.

I was panting and spent by the time he stood and pushed his cock in, sending another wave of tremors through my body. He kicked a chair out from under the table and pulled me back against him, lifting one of my legs onto the chair.

"Fuck, yes." He grabbed my chin and brought my lips to his. He groaned into my mouth as he thrust harder.

My feet and hands were still tingling from my orgasm as a new one built deeper inside me. No other sexual experience compared to this, and I was going to come undone.

His lips ripped away from mine. "Mine," he growled and then bit into my shoulder.

My body lit up like a nuclear bomb, and I stifled my scream with the back of my hand as an orgasm so intense ripped through me I got spots in my vision.

Cole thrust one last time before he spilled inside me. Instinctively, I knew he had just marked me as his, but I didn't care.

He was mine too.

∽

I SMILED as I passed Cole coming back into the house from loading my suitcase into the bed of his truck. He winked, and my neck burned with a blush as he ran back up the steps and disappeared inside the house.

I slid the box onto the tailgate and was just about to head back in to make sure everything was ready to lock up, when a man on a Harley motorcycle pulled into the driveway right behind me.

He took off his helmet and ran a hand through his disheveled, dirty blonde hair that fell to his jaw. A jaw hidden behind a close-cut beard of the same color.

He threw his leg over the motorcycle, put the helmet on the seat, and came toward me with a shit-eating grin that lit up his entire face. Jesus. Who was this guy, the president of a motorcycle gang?

"Uh, hi?" I had never seen him before, but he looked like he knew me. "Can I help you?"

"I'm Silas." He closed the distance between us with an outstretched hand. Shit, this was the other pack leader.

I didn't know what else to do, so I stuck my hand out. If he had sent two guys to kill us, the last thing I wanted to do was to exacerbate the situation by refusing a handshake.

Warmth spread up my arm at his touch, and my eyes didn't leave his darkened baby blues as he brought my hand to his lips and kissed it. His eyes narrowed slightly and then the grin was back.

"Did you just move in around here?" I faked nonchalance as I pulled my hand back and bit my lip. Damn. What was with my reaction to all these men?

"I've lived here all my life. I wanted to invite you to join my pack." He shoved his hands in his front pockets and shrugged. "You should explore all the options available to you."

A growl came from behind me, and before I could even turn, Cole had Silas by the front of his shirt. "What the fuck are you doing here?"

Silas held up his hands in surrender and laughed like being threatened by a growling man wasn't anything new. "Just checking out what's brought Cole Delaney to where he doesn't belong. I definitely see why now." Silas looked over Cole's shoulder at me. "What pack is she from?"

Cole shoved him toward his bike. "She's from back east. Now, leave."

"You always had trouble sharing your toys,

Delaney." Silas stepped forward, and I swore they were so close their noses were touching.

"You sent your betas to kill me." Cole seemed to use all his willpower to hold himself back from punching Silas in the face.

"What pack, Coco?" The grin on his face was just making the situation worse.

I looked around, wondering at what point the neighbors were going to come out and watch the show. Someone would probably catch the display of alpha possessiveness on their doorbell camera and share it all over social media.

"Forest Hill pack." It sounded like a good pack name to me. "Can you stop before the neighbors call the police?"

"I'll give the alpha of *Forest Hill* a call." Silas stepped back and ran a hand down the front of his black shirt before looking at me with a smirk. "Just head west if you decide you want to be around real wolves, bunny."

Bunny? What the hell kind of name was that? My wolf was insulted.

He slid his helmet over his head, never taking his eyes off me, and got on his bike. I put my hand on Cole's arm and squeezed as Silas peeled out down the street.

"I knew this was a bad idea." Cole went to the porch where he left a box. "He's a fucking asshole."

"I thought that title belonged to you." I laughed and then cleared my throat when he frowned at me. "He's the alpha of the other pack, right? What was he talking about sharing toys for?"

Cole put the box he was carrying in the back of the truck and climbed up to strap them in with bungee cords. "We used to be best friends and we literally shared all of our toys. We lived right next door to each other. Then the pack split."

Sounded like a bunch of unnecessary drama to me. Who knew men could have so much? Didn't they usually punch it out, fist bump, and call it a day?

"There are a few more things I want to pack." I walked backward toward the house. "Give me five minutes?"

"Sounds good." He sat down on the tailgate and pulled out his phone. "I should call my betas about Silas making an appearance."

I ran up the steps and went into my office off the entryway, shutting the door behind me. I needed to make sure my friends weren't freaking out about where I was.

I opened my laptop and several email and messenger notifications greeted me. I quickly replied to Jessica, who probably had already tried coming to my house. I told her I was fine and just needed a break. I had been going nonstop since graduating high school and hadn't really had a break.

I opened the messages from Riley and sighed. She was going to be harder to placate. It had been a big change to our friendship when we went to college two hours apart and then when I moved four hours away from our hometown.

Riley: *Your phone goes straight to voicemail.*
Riley: *Your work says you took a leave. What the fuck?*

Riley: *I'm about to get in my car and drive there. Let me know if you're okay!*

The last message was sent the day before. I wondered just how much I should tell her. Yes, she was different like me, but I didn't know what her kind would do if they knew there were others besides them. Plus, I didn't know who might watch her messages.

Me: *It's complicated. I need to go away for a while. I guess we now know why the sheep and goats from that field trip in elementary school hated me so much...*

It didn't take long for the three dots to appear. I hoped Cole wouldn't come looking for me.

Riley: *I'm confused. Why do you have to go away?*

Me: *I've changed. Like you during senior year, except with a lot of hair and a penchant for deer.*

Riley: *Let us help. We can come get you.*

Me: *And end up locked away? No thanks. Don't tell anyone, even the Three Stooges. I'll contact you as soon as I can.*

The door to the office opened, and Cole gave me a look of disapproval. "Ivy, what are you doing?"

I quickly closed out of everything and shut the screen. "Making sure my friends don't call the police or come here looking for me."

He ran a hand over his head and down his face before shaking his head and looking around my office at the photos on the wall. "Are these your parents?"

"Yes." I grabbed my laptop bag and slid it in with the charger. "They died in a car crash on the way to my graduation."

"I'm sorry." His brows arched in concern, and I avoided his stare.

Do not cry.

I cleared my throat and slung the bag over my shoulder. "We should go before I talk myself out of listening to you."

I was too far involved now to turn back.

CHAPTER SIXTEEN

Eli

One of my favorite ways to relax was to garden. With the warmer weather and no sign snow would come again, it was time to clean the flower beds and prepare the garden for spring. Now that my mate would join us, I was even more motivated to make the yard look the best it ever had.

Right after Cole left with Ivy, I set to work weeding, edging, and mowing the front and back. It felt good to feel the chill of the morning give way as the sun warmed the earth.

Sara told me I needed to "woo" Ivy and show her what an excellent mate I was. I was competing against Cole though, and despite him being grumpy at times, he had the whole alpha male thing going for him. What did I have?

Sighing, I shook a bundle of weeds, getting the dirt off. I was the least likely in the pack to find a romantic partner with another wolf. It's just the way it was. My life was the well-being of the pack.

Cole's truck pulled into the driveway as I was scooping up the last of the weeds I had dug out of the flower bed by the front steps. They had been gone all morning, and I was excited to see Ivy's reaction to the work I'd done.

That was until Cole came around the front of the truck and opened Ivy's door. Their scents overwhelmed me, and a growl I couldn't control bubbled up inside me and ripped out of my mouth. "Mine."

I dropped to the ground and shifted faster than I'd ever shifted before. I lunged for Cole just as he shifted mid-leap and we collided. Anger and regret swirled inside me as Cole and I tumbled across the lawn, teeth digging into skin. He'd probably win, but I had to try. Ivy was my mate, and he'd fucked her.

"She's mine!" Cole was pissed as he got me onto my back. I didn't give in and bit his front leg as I thrashed to escape from under him.

"She's my mate!" We circled each other, all teeth and snarls. *"You just couldn't resist getting your dick wet with the new wolf, could you?"*

Cole's growls increased, and he closed in on me. My instincts told me to give in or I was going to get my throat ripped out, but I couldn't.

"I'm the alpha of this pack and-" Cole didn't get to finish because a cold, hard burst of water hit both of us.

We yelped and separated, turning our attention to

where the assault had come from. Ivy was standing with the water hose in her hand, her fingers ready to pull the trigger again.

"Stop it! If this is the welcome I'm going to have to deal with, you can just take me back home right now. Stop acting like toddlers."

I swallowed down a whimper and lowered to my stomach with my ass in the air, my tail wagging. My wolf didn't want to see our mate pissed off at us.

Cole's wolf had a different idea though as he stalked toward her, his body lowered in a position that would have made me tuck my tail.

"Cole, stay the fuck back or I will spray your ass again." Ivy stood her ground and pointed the nozzle right at Cole's face. She had it on full stream blast too, so it would sting.

Cole, being the stubborn alpha he was, didn't listen. One more step forward was all it took for Ivy to squeeze the trigger and hit him with a powerful stream of icy cold water.

He yelped and tripped over his own feet as he scrambled to get away. She didn't let up, stepping closer and trying to squirt him in the nuts.

Hell yeah. That was my fucking mate.

"Damn it, woman! Stop!" Cole shouted as he shifted back and curled into a fetal position on the wet lawn.

Ivy laughed and stopped her assault. "That's what you get for fighting with someone smaller than you."

I wasn't *that* much smaller. I shifted back and stood naked as the day I was born. Her eyes locked with mine and her lips pressed together.

"Ivy." I slowly approached and took the water hose from her, dropping it to the ground. "You're my mate."

Her eyes widened as I cupped her cheek. Did she not feel our connection? She seemed far too shocked by my revelation.

"What do you mean I'm your mate?" She leaned into my touch and didn't pull away. That was a good sign. "Cole's my mate."

My brows furrowed, and I looked over her shoulder at Cole, who was frowning with his arms crossed over his chest.

"But... my wolf..." I leaned in closer to her, which got a growl from Cole. I put my nose against hers. "My wolf is sure you're his mate."

"As is my wolf." Cole came closer and Ivy sucked in a breath. "Her wolf sees me as her mate."

"Ivy?" I pulled back, keeping my hand on her cheek. "What does your wolf say?"

Her frown deepened, and she shut her eyes. "She has only said it once with Cole when we were fighting in the woods. It's like... the more I'm around him, the stronger the feeling gets. With you... it's just a small acknowledgement so far."

"Oh." Letting my hand fall from her cheek, I started to step back, wanting nothing more than to go lick my wounds.

She grabbed my hand and stopped me. "There is something there, though. I've been around Cole more. I'm still working on sharing thoughts with this thing inside of me." She winced. "She did not like being called a thing."

"Two mates? What is going on here?" Cole had moved awfully close to Ivy from behind and put his hands on her arms. "The alpha and the omega? This should be interesting."

Ivy leaned back into his touch and jealousy rose up in me, making me step in closer. She was in the middle of two naked males and it didn't go unnoticed by my cock.

"No more fighting over me. I'm not a piece of meat." She shut her eyes again as we sandwiched her between us. "We'll figure out what's going on before this goes too far and someone ends up getting hurt."

Leaning my head down, I buried my face in her neck and breathed in her scent. She smelled delicious, like fresh dew on flowers right after the rain. I ignored the scent of Cole radiating off her.

A throat cleared and all three of our heads swiveled to find Sara standing in the driveway, leaning against the truck with her arms crossed. She had an amused, yet contemplative look on her face.

"I hate to interrupt this little naked hug fest, but Cole, the betas are calling a meeting." She cleared her throat. "Word spread quickly that you were moving Ivy in without having a vote."

"A vote?" Ivy stepped out from between us, and I immediately felt the loss of being near her. "Is this like *Survivor* and they can vote me off the island?"

"It takes a lot to be voted or kicked out of a pack, but to be allowed in takes the pack council, which is made up of the betas, to agree." Sara opened the back door of the truck and pulled out two pairs of shorts, throwing them at me and Cole. "Put some clothes on. This is too serious to have dicks hanging out everywhere."

"This situation is a little different than when we normally allow others into the pack." Cole pulled on his shorts and put his hands on his hips. "When is the meeting?"

"Right before the pack dinner you scheduled without a reason." Sara raised an eyebrow. "They are not happy with her being here."

I rolled my eyes. The betas always had issues anytime something was out of the ordinary, and Ivy was definitely out of the ordinary.

～

IVY SAID she wanted to be left alone to unpack after we carried her things upstairs. I couldn't say I blamed her after our display of aggression on the front lawn and word that the pack was going to vote on if she could stay.

After leaving a sandwich and chips outside her door for lunch, I went back to the kitchen where Cole was already halfway done eating.

"Can you make me another sandwich? I'm starving after my morning activities." He didn't look up from his laptop, which he had opened in front of him. "Then we need to discuss what happened earlier."

A small part of me wanted to tell him no and to go eat an old sock. Sighing, I squirted mustard on my ham sandwich and put it on his plate before making myself a new one.

I sat down across from him and dug into my sandwich. I'd worked up an appetite from gardening.

After a few bites, I set down my lunch. "I'm sorry. I shouldn't have attacked you."

Cole clicked around a few times on his computer and then shut the screen, giving me his full attention. "My wolf could have ripped your throat out, Elias."

Damn, he was whole naming me.

I picked a small piece of crust off my bread and popped it in my mouth. I knew what could have happened. I'd played the scene over and over in my head already.

"I was acting on instinct and let my emotions get too out of control. My wolf forgot his place." It rarely happened, but when it did it was a reminder that my wolf knew he wasn't *really* at the bottom of the pack; but he wasn't anywhere near the top.

"What if I had been Dante? You could have been really hurt. I knew this was going to be a problem at some point. Your wolf might not be the strongest, but he isn't the weakest." Cole put his wadded-up napkin on his plate. "I think you need to consider letting nature take its course."

"No." Standing, I grabbed his plate and took it to the sink, dropping it a little too hard and causing a piece to chip off. "I'm not going to let Sara be treated like that. She has it hard enough as it is without all the wolves laying into her when they're pissy or need to feel dominant."

We'd had this conversation before, and every time we did, it left me with a bitter taste in my mouth and in a foul mood. Sara tried not to let her disability define her human half, but it affected her wolf half, and being omega would not help it any.

"If someone other than Sara had seen us going at each other like that..." Cole came up behind me and put his hand on my shoulder. "You know it's a struggle to fight our animal's instincts, especially when there are others around."

My grip tightened on the side of the sink. "I know. Which is why I couldn't stop my wolf from going after you. What are we going to do? Your wolf isn't just going to let you share her."

He squeezed my shoulder and then leaned against the counter next to me, a thoughtful look on his face. "I don't think Ivy's wolf is going to let me push you out of the picture. She might not fully recognize you as her mate yet, but you haven't spent as much time with her as I have."

Grunting, I pushed off the sink and leaned against the opposite counter. "Man, she must be something special. I've never heard of one, let alone two mates. Not in real life, anyway."

"Yeah, well, she must have some serious pussy mojo going on then." Cole looked in the sink and then turned on the water to rinse the dishes. He really couldn't stand for them to be left there. "She had a book in her bedroom that had one woman and multiple men as lovers."

"Oh, reverse harem?" I perked up. Some of the other

wolves read a lot too, but not anyone I would freely admit my tastes to.

"Do I even want to know how you know it's called that?" Cole loaded the dishwasher.

"You learn a lot from reading romance. You should try it sometime." Cole was the only one who knew my reading preferences. If anyone else knew, they'd never stop teasing me. "It's a glimpse into the female mind and what she really wants from a man... or men."

"And what's that?" He turned to look at me while drying his hands. "Share this knowledge you've learned; I need all the help I can get."

"Well, uh..." No one had ever asked me for details about what I read, so I said the first thing that came to mind. "Orgasms. Lots and lots of orgasms."

Cole cracked a smile and threw the drying rag at my face. "No, really? I thought you were going to say double vaginal penetration."

"Well, that too." My face was undoubtedly red from embarrassment. "Are we good now?"

"For now." He grabbed his laptop off the table. "Finish your lunch, Eli. You might need your energy for whatever might transpire in a few hours."

Did he mean with the pack meeting or with Ivy?

CHAPTER SEVENTEEN

Ivy

*T*wo mates?

I didn't know what to do with that. I had just come to terms with the fact that Cole was something more than just an alpha. My body was still thrumming from the sex we had and the thought of all the sex to come.

Then there was Eli. I didn't know much about him other than he ranked low in the wolf hierarchy and was Cole's best friend. What the hell was I going to do?

I didn't know what a mate bond felt like, but my wolf preened when I looked at or thought about either of them. The feeling had been strong when I was shifted. Crap, was I going to have sex as a wolf? I shuddered and wished I had my phone to call someone.

I stared at my unpacked boxes, considering my

options. Was I really going to give up my life and live with the pack? I didn't think I had much of a choice, at least until I figured out how to control myself.

Pulling the box closest to me over, I opened it and pulled out a framed picture of me and my parents. Tears welled in my eyes as I remembered how good they had always been to me. There had never been any doubt that they were my parents, and knowing they had kept something so monumental from me was a low blow.

They had twenty-five years to tell me, and they chose not to. It made me wonder if they were hiding something. Was it possible they knew I was something other than human?

Growing up, there had been moments that suggested something was different, but nothing that would have warranted a more thorough investigation of my history. Unless I was missing something.

I put the photo on the nightstand and pulled out the next photo of me and Riley. We had been instant best friends since Kindergarten, when I saw her across the classroom. After finding out she was a siren, I assumed it was some magnetic pull she had, but now I wondered if it was something more.

There was a soft knock at the door, and I almost dropped the picture as I dug through my memories, looking for signs I was a wolf. I put the picture next to the one of my parents and made my way around the maze of boxes and bags. I brought way too much, but I wasn't sure how long I was staying, and it didn't sound like another trip to pack more stuff was in the cards.

Especially after Silas showed up at my house. I didn't even know what to think of that whole encounter. My wolf had been curious.

I opened the door to find Eli standing outside with a sheepish smile on his face. He was taller than Cole but was slimmer and had more of a boyish charm about him. He was probably around my age, or maybe a little younger. His twin sister looked younger than me.

"Hi." Inwardly, I cringed at my awkward greeting. I didn't get nervous around men, but he made me feel a flutter in my stomach.

"Hi." He ran his fingers through his dark hair and looked around me at the unpacking I still had to do. "Do you need help unpacking? We have about an hour before the pack meeting."

"The pack meeting to decide my fate?" I moved out of the way so he could enter. "Just how worried do I need to be?"

"I like to think that we decide our own fate." He walked past me, and his scent hit me. "They've never turned someone away from the pack."

Shutting my eyes, I inhaled deeply, and a strangled whimper came from some place buried deep inside. Jesus, was this what it was going to be like now? If I was going to whimper every time I smelled one of them, my wolf and I were going to have it out.

"You okay?" He put his hand on my arm and my body leaned into it, wanting his hands all over me. "Woah, your eyes just flickered."

"What?" I hadn't even realized I'd opened them. I

stepped away from him, putting a box between us. "Why don't you unpack my suitcase? Most of the clothes are on hangers."

"I'm sorry you had to just up and move in here. It must be a lot to take in." He lifted the suitcase onto the bed, his forearm muscles and veins flexing. "We've never had this kind of situation happen before."

I placed a few books in the nightstand, including my dad's address and phone book. He was old school keeping track of contacts, which was to my benefit. I'd only made it through about half, and without my phone or the Wi-Fi password, I wouldn't be getting much more done.

"Why would my birth parents abandon me?" I threw my stuffed dog I'd had since I was a baby on the bed. "Am I even a wolf from around here?"

Eli hung up a large chunk of my clothes and then picked up Ruff Ruff from the bed. "Are you sure your adoptive parents didn't know about you?"

"I can't be positive, why?" I opened the box that had my panties and bras. Eli's eyes locked onto the handful I pulled out as I transferred them to the top drawer of the dresser.

"This is a handmade wolf. Pretty old too, how long have you had it?" He inspected it, and I dropped a handful of bras on the end of the bed and snatched it away from him.

"Forever." I hugged it to me and then examined it more closely. "I thought it was a husky or malamute." There was no tag with who made it, and my parents had always called it Ruff Ruff.

"Even if it was a dog, it's an interesting choice to give a baby as a plush." He turned back to my bag and his eyes landed on my bras, a blush creeping up his neck.

I grabbed them with a laugh and shoved them in the drawer. "So this mate thing... is it normal to have two?"

"It's not normal to even have one." He finished unloading my suitcase, zipped it closed, and placed it in the closet. "Fated mates are only in books."

"Basically, what you're saying is I'm a freak. I know I look different too." I sighed and punched the bottom of the box I had just turned upside down to break the tape. All it did was make a dent.

Eli slid his nail down the tape and cut it open. I took his hand, meaning to examine it since he'd just shifted a single claw, but a flash of heat spread up my arm and straight to my chest. Our eyes locked, and he wrapped his hand around mine and pulled me against him.

"You aren't a freak." His eyes were dilated, and his voice was gravelly. "You're perfect."

"You're just saying that because you're my-" Before I could finish, he leaned in and his lips brushed over mine. They were soft and tasted like coconut, lavender, and something sweet.

I'd never been so intoxicated by a kiss, and I melted into him, our arms trapped between us and pressing between my breasts. His tongue swiped my lips, and I opened for him, letting him explore my mouth.

A gasp left me as I fell backward onto the bed, his weight and scent pressing me into the soft blankets.

My mind screamed at me to stop because I had just had sex with another man that morning, but my body was telling me other things.

Arching up off the bed, I pressed my breasts against his muscular chest and wrapped my arms around his waist. We fit together like two puzzle pieces, and I was certain that he was something more than just some random guy. He was my mate.

A throat cleared and Eli pulled back, me chasing after his lips and then plopping back on the bed when he sat up all the way and turned his attention to the door.

"Pack meeting is in fifteen." Cole pinched his bottom lip, his eyes not leaving mine. "We should go together."

An awkward silence filled the room as I sat up and adjusted my shirt, which had ridden up almost to my bra line. I wanted to bury my face in my pillows as unease rolled through my stomach.

What were we? Was I cheating on him by making out with Eli? Was sleeping with Cole cheating on Eli? I gave in and fell onto my pillow, burying my face in the cold pillowcase.

"I think you broke her." Cole's voice came closer and the bed dipped, a hand landing on my lower back. "Look at me, Ivy."

Groaning, I rolled over and stared up into Cole's brown eyes. They twinkled with mischief, and I shivered as his hand settled on my stomach. "What?"

"What do you want?" It was asked with so much sincerity that it shocked me into complete silence as I looked between the two of them. "You're the one with the pussy. You have all the power."

So much for sincerity. I batted his hand away, and he threw his head back and laughed, and Eli joined him. Was there some kind of joke I was missing?

"I don't know what I want. I just found out I'm not human and that I have two mates. Who the fuck knows if I'll have more. At the rate I'm going, by next week I'll have twenty of you pawing at my door."

A growl rumbled out of Cole as his face grew serious. "Eli is my best friend. If he was anyone else, I wouldn't be able to stop myself from claiming you just for myself."

"Woah, woah, woah." I scrambled off the bed and crossed my arms. "No one said anything about claiming me. Let's not get ahead of ourselves here. Yes, I feel an intense attraction and pull toward both of you, but it's not so overwhelming where the word *claim* should be used."

Eli looked like he had his tail tucked between his legs. "Maybe the feeling just needs time to develop... like your ability to shift."

"Her ability to shift took twenty-six years." Cole stood and brushed past me. I couldn't tell if he was joking, or if he seriously believed it might take me a quarter of a century to develop the same feelings they had. They were feeling way more than I was. "We're going to be late to the meeting."

The last thing I wanted to do was make a bad first impression.

CHAPTER EIGHTEEN

Ivy

The building that was about fifty feet from the house was not what I was expecting. It was deceptive on the outside, but inside it was practically a football field in size. The trees surrounding the exterior really helped conceal it.

The inside looked like a state-of-the-art training facility for a sports team. At the front, near the entrance, was a lounge area with a projector screen and enough seating for two dozen people. Off to the side was a meeting room with a large conference table that had windows looking out. There were several other doors that were closed that had no windows.

That wasn't even the beginning of it. The rest of the room had gym equipment with plenty of room to throw barbells around. There also was a small area in one corner that was an area for children to play in.

"Geez, does the pack have an NFL team?" I didn't know where to look first, there was so much to take in. "Who pays for all of this?"

There were a lot of people already gathered in front of giant roll up doors at the back of the facility. They were talking and laughing, not seeming to notice us yet.

"Welcome to the Wolves' Den." Cole walked ahead of me and Eli as we started across the room toward a small platform that was in front of a giant spray-painted image of a wolf. "Find a spot near the back so she isn't gawked at."

We separated, and Eli took my hand, guiding me toward the back of where the crowd gathered. "The pack is pretty wealthy, but so is Cole."

"What about the other pack... the WAP?" I snorted at the abbreviation. "They do realize that shortening it is *wet ass pussy*, don't they?"

Eli's face morphed from confused, to slightly amused, to embarrassed. "What's that? Girl slang for being horny?"

"It's a song."

"Never heard of it. The West Arbor Pack is not as well off as we are. As far as I know, most of them work in the city to the west of them. Then there's the rumor about the pack getting mixed up in some criminal activity." Eli put his hand on the small of my back as we weaved through the people gathered and stopped by some gym equipment.

"Does the whole pack fit in here?" I leaned against a metal pole that was part of a pullup and squat rack rig attached to the wall.

"They can if something serious happens, but it's usually just heads of families that come." Eli's hand slipped from my lower back into the back pocket of my jeans. It was an intimate gesture, and my lower belly clenched at the thought of his hands running over my bare ass.

"All men?" I saw one or two women, but most of the people in attendance were male. "*All* the decisions are made by men? I thought wolves would be more progressive."

Overhearing my commentary, a few men turned with raised eyebrows, and Eli made a noise in his throat that wasn't quite a growl but was not a friendly sound. They looked confused and turned their attention back to the front as Cole started to speak.

"We've been called here tonight by my betas to discuss and approve Ivy Taylor joining our pack. She will live in my house and be under my protection from this point forward." His powerful voice made me stand a little taller and my wolf perk up. He was a strong leader, and I liked that. "Does anyone have any objections?"

Dante, who stood on the platform off to the side, cleared his throat. "Where did she come from, and why is she running through the woods challenging betas?"

"She moved to Arbor Falls about eight months ago." Cole held up a hand to quiet the group down when everyone started to talk at once. "The car accident we were in caused her first shift."

Cole was just ripping the Band-Aid right off, and the room exploded into discussion and questions.

Is she dangerous?

I heard her hair is red. Why is she red?

She took down a full-sized buck that was four times her size. How is that possible?

What if she's a spy for WAP?

I felt like someone had thrown me to the wolves and leaned closer to Eli, who was tense as eyes landed on us and the flurry of questions continued.

A shrill whistle rang out across the room, causing me to bring my hands to my ears. Cole lowered his fingers from his lips. "Enough. We are better than this. She is a harmless female who needs a pack."

"I don't agree to this. There's something off about her." Dante crossed his arms and looked across the room, finding me without missing a beat. "We're already dealing with enough from Silas, we don't need to worry about a stray."

Oh, hell no. I was perfectly fine with the slew of questions that had come. I was an outsider, and I was definitely different. But calling me a stray? I wasn't privy to wolf lingo yet, but my wolf's hair bristled at being called a stray.

"Twenty-six years ago, I was abandoned in Arbor Falls. I *am* one of you, whether you like it or not. I might not be normal, but who are you to judge what is normal? You- *we* shift into wolves." My voice was calm as I made my way to the platform. Cole had an indistinguishable look in his eyes, and I wondered if I was breaking a wolf rule by speaking. "Cole and Eli are my mates, and I don't plan on leaving either of them. You are more than welcome to find the door if you have an issue."

Gasps spread across the room, and Cole's eyes flickered as his jaw clenched tight enough to break teeth. Oops. Maybe they wanted to keep the mate thing a secret.

"Mates? Is this true?" Dante looked between all of us. "The three of you?"

"It is," Cole confirmed, not looking away from me. "She's my mate. Eli's too."

Dante narrowed his eyes as he stared down at me. "Mates don't exist. She's tricking you."

I went to take a step forward, but Eli grabbed my hand, pulling me to a halt. That didn't stop my mouth, though. "If I were a female that just rolled over on my back, you'd have no qualms about me staying. Would the pack prefer if I went back to Arbor Falls, shifted in the middle of the street, and bit an old woman crossing the road with her breadbasket? I think not."

Eli snorted and then coughed, covering his laugh. I didn't know why I thought about the grandma from *Little Red Riding Hood* when wolves attacking came to mind, but it seemed fitting.

"Let's vote," Dante demanded. My wolf was beside herself with joy that I'd pissed him off. There was something about Dante that made me want to challenge him.

Cole looked like he was ready to punch Dante. If

the pack voted for me to leave, would he really make me? Despite my resistance, I wasn't stupid. I knew I needed the pack more than they needed me.

"All in favor of Ivy being accepted into the pack, raise your hand," Cole said.

I kept my eyes focused on Dante as his face morphed from smug to pissed off. I didn't need to look to see that most of the pack were raising their hands for me to stay. It was a small victory for me, and I wanted to fist pump but kept it to myself.

"The pack has spoken. Ivy is now a member of our pack." Cole nodded at me, and I smiled up at him. "The meeting is adjourned."

Dante and Cole moved off to the side in a heated conversation, and I turned to Eli, who furrowed his brows as he watched.

"What's wrong?" I put my hand on his arm, needing to touch him.

"I don't like that Dante is against you being in the pack. But the pack decided. Now we feast!" He rubbed his hands together. "Whenever there's a new pack member, the inner circle welcomes them with a cookout. Cole seemed to have already planned to welcome you to the pack, since he already had arranged it."

"Food sounds good. Lately, it seems to be all I can think about." I looked back over my shoulder. "I'm sure this is far from over though."

Eli slung his arm around my shoulders, and we walked out one of the roll up doors into the quickly fading light. It was already getting a little chilly from the sun setting. It disappointed me that my body didn't seem to run hot.

When we got back to the house, Sara was in the kitchen preparing steaks and vegetables for the grill. They didn't have any doubts about what the vote would be, and that made me feel a lot better about the whole situation.

"This looks delicious. Do I have time to go take a shower?" I felt gross from moving boxes and the workout I'd had from Cole earlier in the morning.

"It'll be a while until dinner." Sara smiled at me then looked at Eli. "I've got this handled." She winked and turned back to the sink where she was scrubbing potatoes.

My body prickled with awareness as I went to go up the stairs. Eli was right behind me, and when I stopped and turned at the bottom, I ran right into him with my face.

"Ow." I pulled back and rubbed my nose. "What are you-"

He pulled my hand out of the way and his lips were on mine before I could protest. Not that I wanted to protest him kissing me silly. Not breaking contact, he scooped me up and carried me up the stairs, his tongue sliding against mine in smooth strokes that made my toes curl.

"Eli... what... are..." I tried to get the question out between kisses but was having a hard time even focusing on my thoughts.

"Need you." His lips hovered above mine. "Unless you don't want to."

We had somehow ended up in my bathroom and he set me on the counter. He reached behind his neck and pulled off his shirt. Damn, I had no chill when guys did that.

His body was even more magnificent that I had imagined. He was muscular, but not bulky. His chest was devoid of hair, but he had a dark smattering of dark hair trailing from his bellybutton down into his pants.

"It doesn't bother you I had sex with Cole this morning?" I groaned as he stepped between my legs and kissed my neck.

"No, why would it?" He pulled my shirt off and stood back, rubbing his hand over his lips. "Damn, you're beautiful."

My body heated at his praise, and I reached behind me to unclasp my bra. I let it hang from my index finger, his eyes blazing with desire as he looked at my breasts. "Do you like what you see?" I dropped the bra and jumped off the counter, smiling as his tongue nearly hung out of his mouth.

"Do I like what I see?" His eyes were on my tits as I unbuttoned my jeans. His own jeans looked tight in the crotch area.

"Why don't you take off your pants and turn on the shower?" My jeans pooled at my feet, leaving me only in my panties. There was nothing better than feeling the heat of a male's eyes when you were wearing nothing but a pair of panties.

He bit his lip and turned to the shower, turning it

on with a flick of his wrist before he unbuttoned his jeans and they fell to the floor.

"Commando?" Eli surprised me more and more. I never expected him to whisk me upstairs all horny and wanting, and I definitely didn't expect him to like free balling it.

His ass was tight and just as tan as the rest of his body. It was either his natural skin tone or he sunbathed nude. The thought of seeing him lay out on a deck chair completely naked sent a shiver down my spine.

Kicking his pants out of the way, he turned around, giving me a full view of his strong quads and his cock. *Damn.* Was it a requirement to have a nice dick to be a wolf?

"Do you like what you see?" He winked, and I couldn't stop the giggle that escaped.

"It's not how it looks; it's how you use it." I pushed down my panties and stepped toward him, putting my hand over his already hard as stone cock. "Do you know how to use it, Eli?"

His eyes shut as I brushed my thumb over the head, a bead of pre-cum wetting my finger. "Yes."

Our lips met in a bruising kiss that had me gripping his cock and sliding my hand down his velvety length. He groaned into my mouth, and I invited his tongue into my mouth with parted lips.

Somehow we ended up under the stream of hot water without falling or breaking contact. Pushing him against the wall, I kissed down his jaw, the small amount of stubble tickling my lips. His hand went to the back of my head, stroking my wet hair as I kissed down his neck, nipped at each nipple, and got on my knees.

"Ivy..." I took him all the way to the back of my throat. "Fuck, yes." He made a strangled sounding growl as I pressed my tongue under his shaft.

I sucked the head of his dick before releasing it with a pop. "Show me you know how you use your cock, Eli. Fuck my mouth."

His lips parted in a gasp as I grabbed onto his hips. "I don't want to hurt you."

"When a woman tells you to fuck her mouth, you fuck her mouth." I licked his slit and opened for him.

My pussy ached as he grabbed the back of my head and buried himself in my mouth. A satisfied rumble came from deep within me, knowing he had followed my command, and I pushed the need to dominate to the back of my mind.

"Oh, damn." His moans were throaty as he thrusted into my mouth and I sucked with hollowed out cheeks. "That's so good, yes, I'm going to come."

I pulled back before he could, and he let out a strangled sigh. His cock was red and twitching from my mouth, and I placed a kiss on the tip before standing and bending over with my hands against the shower wall.

"I need you inside me." Spreading my legs, I began rubbing my clit. "Fill me up with that cock."

"Jesus." He ran a hand over the tight curve of my ass and dug his fingers into my hips. "I want to devour you."

"Right now, I need you inside me." I arched my back, and he groaned, running a hand between my legs. "Don't you feel how ready I am for you?"

Eli lined up with my entrance and slowly sank into me. My walls squeezed around him as he began sliding in and out in long, slow strokes. His hand reached around to take over rubbing my clit, and I pushed back with every thrust of his hips, taking him deeper.

"Harder, Eli. Fuck me into the tiles." Pressing my palms into the wall and looking back over my shoulder, I pushed back against him, working my hips in a circle.

"Fuck." His pupils almost took over the entire color of his eye, giving him an intense and deadly look.

Our skin slapped together as he increased his pace, his grunts and my moans filling the bathroom with more than just the sound of the shower.

"Oh, yes, yes!" My orgasm slammed into me as I cried out. I clenched around him as his thrusts stuttered and his hot release filled me.

My body was riddled with aftershocks as he pulled out and spun me around to kiss me. His hands came to the sides of my face, and he pulled away and looked into my eyes. "That was... wow."

I wasn't sure what had come over me. Usually, I wasn't so demanding during sex, but it felt right. "I'm sorry if I was bossy."

"Don't apologize." He grabbed the loofah and squirted some of my body wash on it. "I liked it... a lot."

I closed my eyes as he began washing me. I could get used to this.

CHAPTER NINETEEN

Ivy

When we went downstairs, everyone was outside on the deck and lawn where several heaters and fire pits were going. There were about twenty men and women gathered around in small groups, talking, laughing, and drinking. Most were Cole's betas and higher-ranking wolves. The pack was large, and I was glad it wasn't a major wolf rager after being put through the wringer at the meeting.

I was just about to turn back to grab a jacket when Cole walked out holding one of his in his hands. "Thank you." Our fingers brushed and his hand lingered for a moment before he walked over to a chair and climbed up on it.

It was a sight to behold as all conversations came to a stop and everyone turned in his direction. My wolf was pleased, and I stood a little taller knowing he was mine. Damn, it was a weird feeling having animal thoughts right along with my own.

I slipped on the jacket, closing my eyes and breathing in Cole's rich masculine scent. He was going to have to fight me to get his jacket back.

Eli came and stood next to me, handing me a bottle of beer. He put his arm around my waist and pulled me close, kissing my temple.

"Tonight, we welcome Ivy to our pack." Cole's eyes found mine, and I stared back, butterflies assaulting my insides. "May her wolf and human find a safe place here with us... and with me." He tilted his head back and howled.

The others followed, and then everyone clinked beers and chugged them. I stifled a laugh before chugging my own. I didn't even know where to begin when trying to howl. I'd probably sound like a drowning cat trying to.

The evening passed in a blur, most of my time spent around a firepit. Dante didn't come near me—it surprised me he even attended—but Manny was quite pleasant despite our run-in the night before.

After most of the guests left for the night, there were six of us gathered closely in chairs around a firepit. Eli had stayed close to me most of the night, but Cole seemed distant.

"When are we going to get some ink on you, Ivy?" Manny was across from me and took the last drink of his beer before throwing it into a bin.

"Excuse me?" I looked at him through the flames,

and a grin spread across his face at my expression. "There will be no ink on this virgin skin."

"Virgin skin, eh? Didn't you know? Part of the initiation process is to get Cole's name tattooed on your ass." Laughter broke out around the circle.

"Over my dead body." I snorted at my choice of words and took a long drink from my beer. That had to be what triggered me to shift and had saved my life; the thought was sobering.

"Most of us get our wolf tattooed on our back," Manny said and then stood. "Let me know and we'll fire up my gun." He rubbed his hands together. "I'm going to take off." Two others followed his lead, leaving me alone with Cole and Eli.

Cole was quiet, and I kept stealing glances at him, trying to figure him out. He had seemed chatty all night, laughing and joking with everyone else. As soon as we were in the same conversation zone, he had shut down. It was driving me mad that one minute he was buried inside me and the next he was cold. It was like he had man PMS.

Eli went inside the house to clean up the kitchen, and I couldn't stand the silence any longer. "Is there a problem, Cole?" Might as well get it over with instead of letting it fester. I picked up a few abandoned half-full beer bottles and dumped them over the railing.

"No." He turned off a heater, his back to me, and sighed. "My instinct is to rip out Eli's throat for having his hand in your back pocket and for marking you with his scent."

Biting back a laugh at the *marking you with his scent*

comment, I threw the empty bottles into the recycling bin. "I thought you were fine with it."

"I want to be fine with it. Eli is my best friend." He stepped in front of me as I tried to move past him to grab more bottles. "You also challenged my beta yet again."

I crossed my arms. "I won't be bullied. Your pack members didn't seem to mind me standing up to him. They voted for me to stay."

"The pack members see it as your wolf finding her place. Dante saw it as an alpha letting a woman call the shots. He is traditional in his beliefs on wolf etiquette." Cole stepped forward and wrapped his arms around me, putting his nose in my hair and inhaling. He shuddered, and his arms tightened around me.

He was like a furnace, and I snuggled in against him as we stood on the dimly lit deck. "And what do you see it as?"

"I could tell you how my wolf sees it, but that would just piss you off. We sometimes have different opinions that make me moody." He rubbed his cheek against the side of my head, and as animalistic as the gesture was, I enjoyed it. "I just don't want you to pick a fight you can't win."

"You don't need to worry about me." Breathing in his scent, I shut my eyes, and my muscles relaxed. "Why do you smell so good?"

"I imagine it's because I'm your mate." He pulled back and kissed my forehead. "Let's go to bed. You're sleeping with me tonight."

I groaned. "My vagina has taken a pounding today. Maybe I should sleep in my bed."

He chuckled and wrapped his arm around me, walking me toward the sliding door. "I didn't mean to have sex. Just to sleep."

Imagining him wrapped around me, his face buried in my hair, made me happier than I thought it would.

∼

THE SMELL of bacon and coffee woke me up the next morning. Glancing at the clock on the nightstand, I groaned in disappointment that it was barely seven. I loved sleeping in when I had nowhere to be, and seeing as I was on a leave and with little freedom, sleeping all day sounded right up my alley. But the smell of bacon takes no prisoners, so I pulled myself out of Cole's bed.

After brushing my teeth, I went downstairs to find Cole standing by the stove with no shirt on. His back was to me, his wolf tattoo greeting me, and he was staring intently at the pan on the stove that sizzled and popped. My heart sped at the sight.

"Is the bacon going to escape?" He must not have heard or smelled me coming down the stairs because he jumped at the sound of my voice. I laughed and went to the coffee pot where an empty cup waited that had the phrase 'I Don't Do Mondays' on it in shiny letters. In small type under that was a list of the other days of the week. "Did you get me this?"

"I was going to give it to you at work, but well..." He shrugged and walked behind me to the refrigerator.

He yanked it open, glass bottles clinking together, and pulled out eggs and orange juice.

"Do you like bacon and eggs?" He glanced at me briefly but turned his back to me to crack eggs in a bowl near the sink. His pajama bottoms rode low on his hips, showing the slightest sliver of his boxer briefs.

"There are people who don't like bacon and eggs? Well, besides vegans and vegetarians." Now that I was thinking about it, I was always grumpy when meals didn't include some kind of meat. "Where's Eli?"

"He's already outside gardening. He likes to get it done before we workout." He pulled the bacon out of the pan, setting it on paper towels. Before pouring eggs in the pan, he poured the grease into a bowl. The eggs were going to be delicious. "You should come to the den to workout. There are a few women who do their own workout."

"I don't know if you can handle me working out. I'm a beast in the gym." He snorted, and I gasped. "I'm a division one volleyball champion and was captain of my undefeated intramural team."

"How long has it been since you went beast mode in the gym?" He turned around and handed me two plates with steaming scrambled eggs, toast, and bacon.

My stomach growled as I sat down at the kitchen table, putting Cole's plate where he always sat. "It's been a few weeks since I worked out. With the retirement party, my birthday, and then my almost death, I've been a bit busy."

Cole went to the refrigerator and filled two glasses with ice. As he walked toward the table, I nearly choked on the piece of bacon I had just shoved in my mouth.

I had seen him naked after shifting and after having sex, but the sight of him strutting toward me in pajama bottoms was almost too much. They were barely hanging on his hips, riding just low enough to be indecent, and his muscles flexed as he walked. Besides the V cut that pointed like an arrow into his pants, there were a few raised veins that made my eyes settle there for way too long.

"Normally, I just walk around here naked in the morning, but I figured that might not be conducive to us doing anything except fucking all day. Next time, I'll put a shirt on," he said teasingly. He sat down next to me, poured himself some orange juice, and took a drink, glancing at me out of the corner of his eye. His closeness was making my nipples harden.

"No! I mean…" I shoved a large bite of toast into my mouth to shut myself up. His mouth quirked into a smile. I swallowed the toast and changed the subject. "Do you normally cook?"

"Eli cooks most of the time, but I told him I wanted to cook you breakfast." He took a bite of bacon and closed his eyes as if he was savoring the taste. It was like he was purposely trying to rile me up.

"Who cooked that venison the other night?" *Please say Eli.* I really didn't need any more reasons to find him attractive. I was spiraling head-first into adoration of this male, and I didn't want to go down that road when there were so many uncertainties.

"I did. I enjoy cooking when Eli lets me. What about you? Do you enjoy it?"

"Oh yes, very much so," I replied with a sultry rasp. He meant his cooking, right? I needed a cold shower or a workout. These feelings were making me have impure thoughts. "No, I don't cook. I mean, I can, but what's the point in cooking for one?" I put the back of my hand to my forehead to make sure I wasn't running a fever; my words were like word vomit.

"Well, now you don't have to worry about that." He smiled sheepishly, and my heart melted. I knew asshole Cole was still in there somewhere, but right then, he was pouring on the sweetness. It was the perfect opportunity to try my hand at getting what I wanted.

"When can I have my cell phone back and the Wi-Fi password? I'm about halfway through my dad's contacts to see if any have a connection to Arbor Falls or anywhere around here."

"I'll text Sara and see if she's done adding some precautionary measures to your phone." When I narrowed my eyes at him, he laughed. "Just secure browsing, calling, and texting ability, and a GPS tracker. All of us have it. It's important we know where everyone is in case shit goes down. We only use it in emergencies... like when we crashed. That's how everyone got to us so quickly."

"And if I don't want a GPS tracker on my phone?" My gums started tingling like the canines were about to break through. My wolf did not like the idea of being located so easily.

"Then no phone." His voice was stern, and the

thought about him making a good father popped into my head. I did not need to be thinking about babies when it came to him.

We ate the rest of breakfast in silence as I stewed over my new reality. I could still run. They thought I was all-in; it would be the perfect opportunity to find a set of car keys and run.

The thought of leaving Cole and Eli behind made my wolf growl and my stomach twist into a million knots. I couldn't run.

I finished the last bite of my breakfast and sighed contentedly. So what if my phone had a tracker on it? The food more than made up for the invasion of privacy.

"Go get changed. I'll meet you in the gym." He grabbed our empty plates and took them to the sink.

I went upstairs and changed into black shorts, a strappy sports bra, and a red form fitting racer back tank top. Even though it was cold, I knew I wouldn't be once we started working out. Looking at myself in the mirror, I could tell I had lost some muscle definition in the short stint away from working out.

I threw on a zip up sweatshirt and ran down the stairs, nearly knocking over Sara as I flew off the bottom step. "Woah, hot stuff. Check you out." Sara's hazel eyes swept over me and she wiggled her eyebrows and then grimaced. "You're going to work out? Yuck." She pressed my cellphone into my hand. "A gift."

Examining it, I couldn't stop from scrunching my

nose in distaste. "Thanks. Is it now complete with stalker chip and everything?"

Sara laughed and followed me out onto the deck. "It will only be used if needed. We all have them in our phones. No biggie." Sure it wasn't a big deal for her, she'd grown up this way. It made me feel powerless and not trusted.

"Does the pack always workout together? Why aren't you in gym clothes?" She was wearing leggings, an oversized sweater, and boots.

She followed me down the deck steps and across the lawn. My legs were freezing, and I regretted wearing shorts, the cool air making goosebumps rise on my skin.

"I try not to embarrass myself or remind the pack I'm the weakest link." There was sadness in her voice, and I wanted to hug her, but then she laughed. "Girl, you are going to get eaten alive in there. I think I'll stay and watch for a while."

We walked in the roll up door and it was like the air had been sucked out of the room when I entered. About a dozen sets of eyes landed on me and Sara and did a slow sweep of us.

Crap, maybe I should have worn capris or pants instead. Before I could talk myself out of it, I walked right up to the giant whiteboard where they gathered to see what was planned.

"We have a workout planned for the women over near the kid zone," Manny said as he stepped up next to me with his arms crossed.

I turned and looked to where he was referring. Five

women were gathered chatting with Sara, who had made a beeline for them almost immediately. I glanced over at Manny and then back at the board, which had a warmup, weightlifting, and a workout.

I had a distinct feeling that these wolves treated women as less than equals with pretty much everything. I understood they were part wild animal and with that came thoughts that might seem like they were stuck in the past, but it got under my skin. Hell, regular human beings treated women differently.

However, I wasn't raised in the way of the wolf, so I decided right then and there that their rules didn't apply to me.

CHAPTER TWENTY

Eli

To say I went to bed disappointed was an understatement. The night before, Cole had come in with Ivy and they finished helping me clean up the kitchen. After a quick peck on the lips, she followed Cole up the stairs, holding his hand.

Having the same mate was going to be harder than I thought. I saw how moody Cole had gotten when I'd had my hands on her during the pack meeting and then at the cookout. If he wanted, he could easily take me out of the equation.

When I woke up and went to make breakfast, Cole was already at the stove. Her scent lingered on him, and it took everything in me not to run upstairs, bust down the door to Cole's bedroom, and take her to my room instead.

So, I did what any man would do and went and hid in the garden. I didn't really need to do anything besides make sure rodents weren't bypassing my safeguards. I hated when the squirrels dug up my root vegetables or buried their damn nuts in my pots. If cats liked us, I'd get a few of them to chase the assholes away.

The greenhouse was already heating up nicely as I opened the door and stepped inside. My aromatic herbs hit my nostrils, and I breathed deep.

Wolf.

There was a faint scent of an unknown wolf by the other door into the greenhouse. I could barely smell it in human form, but it was there. Walking across the room, I sniffed again and winced. Whoever had been inside my greenhouse needed a bath.

I texted Dante since he was in charge of protecting our territory. It was probably nothing. Our land was well protected.

After watering a few plants that were a bit dry, I headed to the Wolves' Den for a workout. It didn't take much for us to stay in shape, but not strength training and conditioning our human halves made our wolves cranky.

"No, this workout looks just fine. I appreciate your concern though." Ivy's voice was easily recognizable as I approached the roll up door.

It took a second for my eyes to adjust from being out in the sun, but when they did, a low rumble built in my chest.

What the hell is she wearing?

The entire pack—the thirteen that were in the gym—were staring at her long, bare legs and her gorgeous ass highlighted by the skin-tight black shorts she had on.

Jesus.

Cole clapped me on the shoulder from behind, and I nearly jumped out of my skin. "Why are you standing here-" He fell silent, and his grip tightened. "She can't be serious. It's like she's wearing underwear!"

She must have heard him because her head turned, and she winked. Cole let go of my shoulder, and we walked to where she was standing with Manny, looking over the workout he had programmed for us.

"Ivy, what are you doing?" Cole crossed his arms, and I followed suit.

"Preparing to workout. What are you doing?" Ivy unzipped her hoodie and slid it off. My eyes went wide enough for my eyeballs to pop out. It wasn't that I didn't recognize the outfit she was wearing was normal workout attire, but I didn't want the horny bastards in the gym to be staring at her in her shorts and skintight tank top. She might as well have been wearing nothing.

Cole cleared his throat. "This workout is pretty rough."

"I see that." She dropped her sweater near the wall and left us staring after her.

Manny laughed. "Good luck with that one. She is something else."

"You can say that again," Cole muttered as he watched her walk away. We both let out growls as everyone else had the same idea.

"I'm going to go workout next to her. Make sure she's safe." I went to the middle of the workout area where Ivy was already setting up her equipment.

Cole made a few grumbles, but didn't follow. Since he was the alpha, it was important he be front and center so others would push themselves. It was rare he was outlifted or beat during a timed workout.

"This isn't something to take lightly, Ivy. You could get hurt." I didn't want to sound like a complete chauvinistic pig, but was afraid it sounded like that anyway. "We've been doing this style of workout for a while. One rep with bad form and you could really injure yourself."

She put two ten-pound plates and collars on the ground next to the empty bar. She frowned at me and shook her head in disbelief. "I know what I'm doing. Arbor Falls does have some things."

"The bar is twenty kilograms, not pounds." I knew as soon as it was out of my mouth it was a mistake. Ivy narrowed her eyes and opened her mouth to say something, but then Manny yelled for us to warm up.

She ran out the door after the others to do a few laps around the building. I followed and tried not to watch the way her hamstrings and calves flexed as she ran. She was in good shape.

I sped up until we were shoulder to shoulder. "I'm sorry."

"You're sorry? You are all sexist pigs! Why is it so hard to believe a woman can lift heavy shit and keep up with the boys? I bet you a blow job I will beat half these fuckers, including you."

Woah. My dick twitched in my pants at how confident she was... and about the blow job. "So, if you beat half of them... so, six of them, then you get what? Oral?" Either way, it was a win for me.

"Yes, and if not, then I will drop to my knees and deep throat you until your eyes roll back and you scream my name loud enough for all the forest creatures to hear."

I tripped over my own feet and fell just before we rounded the corner. My body skidded across the dirt and gravel where we were.

"Oh, shit. Are you all right?" She ran back to me. "Ouch."

I sat up and scooted against the side of the building, my knees, hands, and arms burning and bleeding. My pride was already gushing blood everywhere. How embarrassing. "I'll be fine."

Yeah, I'd be fine if I didn't melt into the ground first. I wasn't clumsy at all. In fact, the last time I'd fallen had been when I was a young cub just learning to walk. Mention of a deep throat was dangerous to my health.

"Let's get you to the house to clean up." She helped me stand, and I winced as the skin near the abrasions on my legs pulled tight.

"I got it; you can just go workout." Really, I just wanted some privacy so I could let a few tears fall. I wasn't above crying if something hurt like a son of a bitch.

She put her hand on the small of my back and guided me along the walkway to the back deck. "Let me kiss it and make it better."

A snort and then a groan escaped as we climbed the few steps to the deck. We both froze at the top step when a growl came from behind us. We turned, and as soon as I saw and smelled the male at the bottom of the steps, I pushed Ivy behind me.

It had been a while since we had a stray wolf who wandered into our territory, but they were dangerous and unpredictable. He had been in the greenhouse, which meant at some point he had shifted to open it or he was a highly skilled wolf.

"Hey there, my friend. Why don't you shift so we can have a friendly conversation?" I showed him the palms of my hands, which was a sign I wasn't a threat.

A snarl so ferocious ripped from his throat that Ivy let out a small squeal behind me. I could hear the music blaring from the den, so I wasn't sure if anyone from the pack had heard the snarl. If they did, the wolf was a goner. Especially if Cole got to him. We didn't tolerate aggressive wolves who couldn't control themselves.

"Eli, maybe let me try?" Ivy put one of her hands on my arm and looked around me. "He's scared."

"He was in my greenhouse. He's not too scared to come right up to the alpha's house." The wolf's head tilted, and he lowered into a position to jump.

Protect.

We collided midair as my body shifted, and we toppled onto the grass. I had one thing on my mind, and she was currently running to the den to get help.

It was a matter of seconds before the male got me on my back and put his teeth against my throat. He didn't bite though; he just breathed deeply and growled.

I whimpered and wished I could tell him I wasn't going to hurt him. Instead, I turned my head slightly and licked his snout. That apparently did enough to snap him out of his rage because he backed up, his eyes wide.

A snarl came from behind me, and I knew exactly whose. Cole was pissed. He didn't even communicate with me through the pack connection, he just jumped over me and circled the male who was not looking as tough now.

"Cole, he let me go. He looks sick." I didn't know how much of the display of aggression toward me Cole had seen, but judging from his stance, he'd seen a lot.

"He was going to kill you."

The male blinked rapidly and then collapsed onto the ground. I tried to rush forward, but a hand clamped down on my neck.

"Easy does it." Dante squeezed a little too hard for my liking, and I considered turning and biting him in the nuts. Instead, I shifted and ducked away from him. I'd probably pay for that move later when we were both shifted, but I was used to it.

Dante used to be a good friend growing up, until he took over his father's beta position. It was like all the fun was sucked out of him the second he bested his father in a fight.

"Cole, he's sick. Let's get him to the basement so we can watch him and give him some food." Approaching slowly, I squatted behind the wolf and ran a hand down his side. "He's emaciated."

A half growl, half whimper came from the poor guy, but then he shut his eyes. What the hell had happened to him?

Cole shifted and put his hands on his hips. "I don't want a feral stray in the house with Ivy."

"It's not like he can escape from the cages you have." She thankfully stayed back. "There aren't any other options? Imagine being through whatever the hell he's been through and waking up on a cold concrete floor, shackled. I know the feeling well, and he's clearly been through worse."

Continuing to run my hand across the wolf, I agreed. He had only attacked because he was scared. His reaction to me licking him was enough evidence of that. If he meant harm, he would have bitten off my snout for that.

"We can put him in my room," I offered with a slight cringe. I knew it was going to be a no go, but I had to try.

"That's the stupidest thing I've ever heard come out of your mouth." Dante marched over and scooped the wolf up. "Either he goes in the basement, or we drop him off outside our territory."

Without another word, he and Cole went into the house with the wolf passed out in Dante's arms.

CHAPTER TWENTY-ONE

Xander

*M*ine.

CHAPTER TWENTY-TWO

Ivy

I wasn't happy about the wolf being locked in the basement when he so clearly was ill. While Eli went in the house after Cole and Dante, I went and got my sweater, put my equipment away, and made myself comfortable on the hammock on the deck.

My phone was a mess of notifications, emails, and text messages. I never realized just how many I regularly got.

Riley: *I'm still not convinced you're okay. Jax told me to stop worrying, you're a big girl.*

Me: *He's not wrong. I have my phone back now.*

Riley: *What did you mean by you liked deer?*

Me: *Do you remember how in junior high you were team Jacob, and I was team Edward?*

Riley: *Of course. We had shirts and water bottles. I might still have that shirt somewhere...*

Me: *I should have been team Jacob. I can relate to him better.*

It was the only way I could think to tell her I was a wolf shifter without saying it outright. I didn't want to take the chance that someone might watch both of our phones.

My phone immediately started ringing, and I picked up with a laugh. "Before you say anything... my phone has spy stuff on it and who the hell knows what yours has on it."

"Jax knows if he does something to my phone, I'll bite his nipples so hard he'll cry." Damn, she was vicious and had only gotten more so with age. She would absolutely do that if it came down to it.

"That's way too much information, Ri." I laughed and then blew out a frustrated huff of air. "I need to stay here for a while and figure things out."

"And you're sure you can trust these people? Do you know who your biological parents are? It seems like a pregnancy would be pretty hard to miss in a small town. Especially if you're team Jacob."

"No one has said anything yet, but I don't think word has spread far. It doesn't help that there is another group, and they don't get along with each other." I shut my eyes as the sun beat down on my face. "I also kind of have two boyfriends now."

"Holy shit. Welcome to the club!" I heard male voices and a giggle from Riley. "We're getting ready to leave. Call me or text me to check in. We can come get you if you need us to."

"Thanks, Ri."

We hung up, and I got out of the hammock without falling on my ass. Dante opened the slider and stepped out of the house.

"How's the wolf?" I slid my phone in my sweater pocket and gave him a friendly smile. I'd kill him with kindness if I had to.

"Probably going to cause us a lot of problems. Taking in strays is bad for the pack." He purposely walked close to me as I headed for the door and bumped into my shoulder.

My teeth came out. "What the fuck is your problem, Dante?"

His laugh made the hair on my arms stand on end. I hoped it was my human hair and not wolf hair sprouting. "You're my problem. Look at you, you can't even control your wolf! You must be a good fuck for Cole to risk the members of this pack over."

My nails dug into the palms of my hands as I clenched my fists. It was taking everything in me not to rail on him. The desire to put him on his back was so strong I rushed into the house without a word or a glance in his direction.

Dante was going to be a problem, and my wolf wanted nothing more than to put him in his place. I shut my eyes and took deep breaths, counting backward from ten as I stood in the kitchen.

Feeling out of control of my emotions was foreign,

and I didn't like it at all. Was this what all wolves went through?

"Ivy?" Eli came from the hallway and approached slowly. "Sweetie, your hands are dripping blood."

I looked down and quickly unfurled my fists, revealing claws instead of fingernails. "Sweet baby fawn, what the fuck?"

He took me by the wrists and guided me to the sink where he turned on the warm water. "What caused this?"

I winced as the water ran over my palms. "Dante."

He hummed and grabbed a clean towel out of a drawer. "Dante can be hard to deal with." He turned off the water and wrapped my hands. "It shouldn't take these long to heal. I'm already healed from falling earlier. Did you have injuries growing up?"

My eyes went wide, and I pulled my hands away from him, ripping the towel off and staring at my hands that only had faint scratches instead of the gouges they had when I put my hands under the water. "I've been hurt before and it never healed this quickly."

"Before their first shifts, pups are most vulnerable. The first shift happens around twelve years of age." He ran his fingertips over the palms of my hands, and I shivered. "You need to calm down. That's why your teeth and claws are still out."

"I need..." I pulled my hands away and shook them like that would get them to go back to normal. My wolf was clawing to get out. "I need to run."

"Maybe we should-"

Before he could finish, the change tore through me,

shredding my clothes. I would not be buying expensive workout attire anymore, that was for sure.

My paws hit the hardwood floor and made a pleasant clicking sound when I moved. With my nose to the floor, I dashed around the island with a yip. Man, it was slippery as fuck, and I nearly slid into a kitchen chair.

"Ivy, I'll go for a run with you." Eli was already removing his clothes, and I barked.

Oh, wow. This is fun.

I did it again and ran to the couch, jumping onto it. Now, I understood why dogs got on the furniture. It was much better than being on the hard ground. I jumped down, and as soon as my feet hit the plush rug, the urge to roll around on the soft fabric was too strong.

I flopped down and began twisting and rubbing my back on the soft surface, my legs flailing in the air as I scratched an itch right in the center of my back. *Shit, this feels amazing.*

"What the hell is going on—oh, for fuck's sake." Cole was standing at the end of the hall and started laughing. "No wolves in the house."

I jumped up and ran to him, sticking my nose right in his crotch and inhaling. *Mate.* He pushed my snout away, and I growled at him.

"Sorry, Alpha." Eli was fully naked now, and I was so excited he was going to join me I danced my front paws around on the floor and let out more elated wolf noises. "Join us?"

Eli shifted, and Cole let out a slew of curses about

hair getting everywhere. The only natural thing to do was to shake out and send hair flying.

Cole went to the slider and opened it. "Come on. Let's go for a run."

I skidded across the floor and nearly knocked him over as I bolted out the door, sending a howl up as I went. It was so freeing to be in my wolf form.

"I'll race you to the back trees." Cole's voice was in my head, and I jumped slightly at the intrusion as he ran behind me down the steps with Eli.

"It's not a race if I'm going to smoke your ass." I sprinted, my feet pounding the grass and my breaths deepening. My tongue threatened to come out as I pushed my body to go faster.

Cole caught up to me, edging just in front. He was a magnificent beast, with rippling muscles and a powerful stride. He just beat me by a hair, and we slowed as we got into the trees.

"You pushed yourself too hard at the beginning. We have more endurance than a human, but you can burn yourself out quickly."

I looked over at Eli with his tongue hanging out of his mouth, his ribs extending and retracting as he panted from the race. *"Can Eli hear me?"*

His head popped up, and he stared at me. *"What?"*

Cole spoke at the same time. *"No. Only I can have a line of communication with each person. It's an alpha thing."*

"You can hear me?" I stepped closer to him. "But... Cole just said..."

Eli suddenly dropped to the ground and rolled onto his back, showing me his belly. *"My alpha."*

I looked over my shoulder at Cole, who had his lip pulled back in a silent snarl. *"Cole, what's happening?"*

"I don't know." His voice was in my head, but his wolf growled.

My wolf pulled me forward, and I hovered over Eli, my snarl filling the forest. My jaws opened, and I bit into the fur at his neck but didn't break his skin. He whimpered, and I let go.

"What just happened?" I backed up, looking between both of them.

"My wolf wanted in your pack." Eli was still on the ground, but had rolled over to lie on his stomach, placing his head on his front paws and looking at me with glossy eyes. *"Now I have two alphas."*

"Let's run before my wolf loses his shit." Cole ran at breakneck speed into the forest before either of us could respond.

"It was such an overwhelming feeling." Eli crawled toward me on his stomach. *"Cole's still my alpha too."*

I didn't like it one bit. I had no desire to be in charge of a pack. My wolf balked at that. *"Let's go."* Sniffing the air, I ran after Cole's scent.

The forest was beautiful during the early spring. The animals were active, and the trees were vibrant. I used to think fall was the best time of year with the bright colors as leaves turned, but looking at the forest from a different perspective changed that.

Spring meant life.

Cole's scent took me to the base of a tree and then it stopped. Where the hell did he go?

Eli shifted and laughed. "Really, Cole? The treehouse?"

I looked up and sure enough, there was a treehouse hidden in the branches. How was I supposed to shift?

Backing away from the tree, I thought about being myself again. Nothing. I shut my eyes and pushed. Nothing.

I whined as Eli began climbing the rungs of the ladder I hadn't even noticed.

"Push the wolf back," Cole said from above. "You might have to be stern."

Push her back? Ugh. That made no sense. I *was* the wolf. I closed my eyes again and focused on figuring out where she was. It wasn't like I could see her and just grab her by the scruff of her neck.

Just let me shift, damn you!

My skin tingled, and I latched onto that feeling and pushed with all my might, landing on my hands and knees on the forest floor.

"That was crazy." I needed to practice because not being able to go back and forth easily like everyone else could was dangerous.

"Now, get your ass up here." Eli was standing next to Cole, and they both had grins on their faces. "We haven't been here in years."

I climbed the ladder, which went right up into the treehouse. "Wow." I looked around the space that was the size of a small bedroom and had the trunk of the tree running straight up the middle. It was dusty, but oddly clean for them not coming to it for a few years. "What do two grown ass men need with a treehouse?"

"We used to come here when we were teenagers to look at porn magazines and jack off," Eli confessed. Cole smacked him in the back of the head. "I mean, we came here to play with our G.I. Joes."

I rolled my eyes. "You two jacked off together? That's hot."

Both of them blushed, and I laughed. Those dirty dogs.

The room was all wood, but had window hatches on each wall that could open. In one corner there was a small table pushed up against the wall with two chairs, and in another corner were two heavy duty plastic totes stacked on top of each other.

"Is this your porn collection?" I opened a lid, and inside was a ton of Legos, action figures, and toy cars.

"The porn collection is long gone." Cole crossed his arms over his chest. "We need to talk about what happened."

"Oh?" I moved the box and opened the second one, which was packed with military style blankets. I took one out and smelled it. "Surprisingly, this doesn't smell musty."

I unfolded it and wrapped it around myself. Cole frowned as I avoided his question. I honestly had no clue what had happened. It wasn't me who had proclaimed I was an alpha.

"I couldn't stop myself." Eli kept his head down as he grabbed another blanket from the container and tried handing it to Cole, who shook his head. "What's so wrong with having two alphas?"

Cole stared at me. "Nothing, but..."

"But you're worried the betas are going to be pissed. Namely, Dante." Eli wrapped the blanket around himself and sat down in a chair at the table. "I don't see how you're going to stop her wolf from challenging them. You've already seen it's in her nature."

"We're getting way ahead of ourselves here. I barely even became a wolf, and as soon as I get this under control, I'm moving back to my house and going back to work." Cole had me pinned against the tree trunk before I could even finish what I was going to say.

A low rumble came from somewhere deep inside him, but I stared straight into his eyes. His alpha posturing needed to be taken down a peg or two.

"Your place is here. With me. With Eli. You can't move back to your house." His tone held a finality that made my wolf bristle.

I blinked at him. "I won't allow you to tell me what to do. Unless you have some kind of mind-control mojo, I don't follow commands I don't agree with." My fingers itched, and I shut my eyes. "Now, back up before my wolf comes out and bites something you don't want bitten."

His warmth left me, and I stayed leaning against the tree trunk until the tingle was gone. I was willing to stay to learn what I needed to, but they couldn't expect me to give up my entire life. I had a career and friends that were like family to me. I could be their mate or whatever while going about a normal life.

"What Cole was trying to say is it's dangerous to not be in a pack. What if you got injured and ended up in a hospital? Shifting or healing like we do would lead to a lot of questions. There have been wolves who have disappeared, Ivy. We don't know where they end up, but something tells me that the government does, in fact, know we exist, just not to what extent." Eli's eyes were sympathetic as he stood and came toward me. "The fact that you somehow went undetected for so long is unbelievable."

He pulled me into a hug, and I snuggled against him. "I'm a freak," I joked.

"Unless you're referring to yourself as a freak in the sheets, that's nonsense." Eli ran his hand up and down my spine.

"That was a terrible joke." Cole was sitting at the table now, with his arms crossed in what I realized was his all-business alpha pose.

"If we're talking about freaks in the sheets, let's talk about this porn shack in the sky. Did you ever bring chicks up here?" I didn't know a damn thing about teenage boys and their hormones, so I wasn't going to bring up that they used to jack off together.

"No." Eli's cheeks turned rosy, and I narrowed my eyes, wondering what that reaction was about.

"Once." Cole smirked. "Does that bother you, alpha?" He stood and stalked forward, a glint in his eye. Eli backed up so Cole could take his place. "There's only one way for me to get the memory out of my head."

He traced my bottom lip with his finger, and I forgot all about his macho alpha behavior from earlier. "How's that?"

"Create a new memory." His lips brushed across

mine and my arms looped around his neck, dropping the blanket and pressing my naked chest against his.

His hands grabbed my waist and his fingers dug in as he deepened the kiss and pushed me back against the tree trunk. I had different plans than him fucking me against a scratchy tree and pushed at his chest.

With his eyes never leaving me, I picked up the blanket and laid it on the floor. "Lay down."

"Excuse me?" The corner of his mouth turned up as he crossed his arms. He wasn't fooling me. His dick was nearly weeping with how hard it was.

"You heard me. On your back, alpha." Something about these men made me want to be in control.

He looked from me to Eli, who was sitting as stiff as a board at the table, his fists clenching the blanket he had draped around himself. Cole grabbed his dick and gave it a solid pump before doing as I asked.

My core clenched at his compliance.

"Should I leave?" Eli's lips twisted to the side. "Or..."

I sauntered over to him, swaying my hips extra for their benefit, and kissed him before putting my lips against his ear. "Stay right here until I'm ready for you. You have the perfect view for what I'm about to do." He groaned as I took his earlobe between my teeth and bit it gently.

I turned back to Cole, who was watching intently with his dick in his hand. There had been no reason for the small bit of doubt that had creeped up about being with both of them at the same time. They might not have said they were fine with it, but their reactions spoke loud and clear.

Kneeling at Cole's feet, I pushed his legs until he grabbed his knees. "Woman, what are you doing?"

"Taking what's mine." Shocked he'd let me put him in such a compromising position, I waited a moment to see if he was going to have an issue with it.

"Well, do it. Unless you're too nervous." His cock jerked and a bead of pre-cum dripped down the side.

"Just wanted to make sure I wasn't about to hurt your ego any." I grabbed the base of his cock and stroked him a few times. "Are you ready for me to rock your world, baby?" I purposely made myself have a lower voice.

He laughed. "Either fuck me, or come sit on my face. Your choice."

I positioned myself over him and eased him inside me, groaning as I sheathed him to his hilt. Bracing my hands on his legs, I lifted off him before sliding back down.

"Fuck me." Cole shut his eyes, and his lips parted as I took him inside me over and over again.

I glanced over my shoulder at Eli, who had been quiet since I left him panting for more. His cock was in his hand, and he stared at my pussy sliding along Cole's cock.

"Do you like what you see?" I increased the pace, and Cole gasped. "Are you imagining what it would feel like if I were riding your cock right now?"

"I'm going to fucking come if you don't stop with that," Cole bit out.

"Come here, Eli."

Eli stood, his cock standing at attention against his

lower abdomen and leaving glistening pre-cum in its wake. "Where should I..." He stood to the side, and I shook my head.

"Lay down. Ass to ass." His eyes widened, but then he was down on the blanket, mirroring Cole's position, holding his legs on his back. "Closer... unless either of you are uncomfortable..."

"Just do what she says," Cole growled, letting his feet rest flat on the ground and reaching up to pinch my nipples.

Eli wiggled closer until their balls were almost touching, and my pussy squeezed around Cole. I wanted them both so badly it hurt. I'd never done the Amazon position before, but seeing both men on their backs in such a submissive position made it a new favorite.

I slid off Cole and planted both feet on the floor, using his legs to keep myself steady as I lowered myself backward onto Eli. "Oh, wow." He hit me in the right spot, and I nearly saw stars.

Cole pumped his cock, breathing heavily, and then moved his cock to rub against my clit. My legs trembled as my orgasm pulsated through me, squeezing Eli until he cried out and he spilled inside me.

He pulled out, and Cole flipped me, my hands landing on Eli's thighs, his cock glistening right in front of my face. I cried out and dug my fingers into his skin as Cole didn't hold back, his thrusts fast and hard.

His hand wrapped around my torso and pulled me back against him, both of us on our knees, and his fingers went to my clit. He licked the shell of my ear, and I trembled. "Let our omega see his alphas come together."

A scream ripped from my throat as my orgasm came from all directions. I clenched around him and he buried his face against the back of my neck, groaning as he came along with me.

Everything tingled as the last tendrils of pleasure coursed through my body and an overwhelming need to cry made my eyes burn.

"Ivy..." Eli got to his knees in front of us and cupped my cheek as I gulped in breaths of air. "What's wrong?"

"Nothing. That was just really fucking intense." I laughed as Cole's heat left me.

Eli helped me up, and Cole cleaned me with the blanket. "I'll have to ride back out here on a quad and grab the blankets to wash."

I felt a little awkward standing in the middle of a treehouse, naked and dripping still. "We should go. It's getting late." I looked at the trapdoor, which we'd left wide open.

After climbing down, Cole began pulling a rope that was the same brown as the tree and the ladder lifted out of view, lifting parallel to the bottom of the treehouse.

"Now I think we can call it a porn shack in the sky." I laughed just before shifting to my wolf without another thought.

CHAPTER TWENTY-THREE

Xander

The scent of her overwhelmed me as I pushed through the darkness that wrapped around me like an old friend. A very toxic, suffocating friend. My entire body felt like it had been run through a meat grinder and then hot glued back together. Maybe it had.

I forced my eyes to open and my body stiffened, seeing the gray concrete and bars surrounding me.

No. Not again.

How had they gotten me? I thought I had killed them all.

They'd taken everything from me. My pack. My desire to fight. My life.

The faintest sounds of footsteps overhead drew my attention to the direction they were walking in. I was in a basement and the footsteps were going toward the stairs leading down.

I wouldn't let them touch me again. I'd die before I let that happen.

Rolling over, I winced as my body rejected the movement. Chains scraped across the concrete, and I looked down at my front feet. Chained once again, but not muzzled.

That would be their mistake.

The door opened and scents hit me that confused my wolf. Why would my mate be fucking two other males while I was chained in a basement?

Her rainbow striped socks came into view first, followed by tight jeans that looked melted on her body. I pushed against my wolf to shift, but his hold was strong. I let him be in charge too long.

She was wearing a loose, peach colored sweater with her red hair falling over her shoulders. She was magnificent, and she was mine.

"Hey, you're awake." She stopped at the bottom of the stairs and looked back up them, pulling her bottom lip between her teeth. She cautiously approached the cage, and I didn't move an inch. I didn't want her to see that I couldn't even protect myself.

She had a reusable water bottle under one arm, and in her hand was a plate. My mouth was already watering with the smell that wafted from it.

"Are you hungry?" She laughed nervously. "Of course you are. When I first woke up down here I was starving and all they gave me was a sandwich. Can you believe that bullshit?"

They'd locked my mate up too?

A growl tore from me and she stepped back with wide eyes. Damn it, I scared her.

Whining, I changed course and crawled forward toward the bars. Was she going to go get the men now that I'd frightened her? Why was she even here in the first place?

"Why don't you shift back? I have some cooked steak here for you. You might like it better as a human." She knelt down just out of range of where I would be able to touch her. "They aren't going to let you out of here until you shift."

Of course they weren't.

My belly ached with the need for food. I was sure my human form was in even worse shape. My wolf had locked him out for weeks, or maybe it was months. Why shift when my wolf could open doors and get along perfectly fine without me? It was easier this way; the pain less.

I sniffed the air and moved a little closer, my eyes on the plate she set down. Once my nose was just between the bars and could go no further, she smiled.

"Oh, geez. I totally just had the urge to say *good boy* to you. That's probably a wolf shifter faux pas." She certainly was chatty. I wasn't used to the auditory stimulation.

She pushed the plate right up to the bars, but I couldn't get the meat that way. A line formed between her eyebrows, and she pulled the plate away. She seemed to concentrate on her thoughts, and then she nodded, picked up a piece, and put it in her palm.

"I know this is stupid of me, but I'll heal, right? I don't want you to have to eat off the dirty floor." She laughed nervously.

The thought of biting her repulsed me. She moved closer and stuck her hand out as I stepped back so her hand could come through the bars. She had really nice hands, hands that would feel great rubbing the spot behind my ears I could never get.

I took the piece of meat gently off her hand and swallowed it down without chewing. My mate grabbed another piece and continued feeding me through the bars of the cage. When the meat was all gone, she turned the glass plate sideways and put it through the bars, letting me lick the juices and tiny meat pieces that were left.

"If they come down here later to feed you, pretend you didn't have leftover steak, okay?" She poured water from the bottle she had onto the plate and I lapped it up. "Cole said I'm not allowed down here alone, and if he finds out I didn't listen..."

I growled again, not liking the sound of Cole. If he laid a hand on her—

The door upstairs opened, and she sucked in a breath. I pulled myself to my feet on wobbly legs, willing to defend her if Cole came at her. I didn't know how with being locked up, but I would.

But I knew the scent coming down the stairs. It was the wolf who tried to lick me. I growled as he came completely into view at the bottom of the stairs.

"Ivy, we told you not to come down here alone. He's

dangerous." He didn't sound mad, but the worst type of anger was the kind that lurked silently.

I'll show you dangerous. I showed my teeth and my hair bristled.

"He's not. Maybe he needs human contact to want to shift back. Who knows how long he's been like this." She stood and crossed her arms. "You brought him a blanket."

He shrugged. "Well, since Cole said he can't sleep in my room, I figured I'd bring my room to him."

I really didn't like the sound of this Cole guy. My head tilted to the side in curiosity as he hugged a blanket to his chest. It had been a long time since I'd felt the comforts of a blanket.

"But he's too dangerous for me to come visit and feed when there are bars and chains keeping him away from me? Unbelievable. No wonder both of you are single." My mate defending me made me puff out my chest. Normally my wolf would balk at the idea, but desperate times and all.

"We aren't single anymore, are we?" He gave her a lopsided smile that was both infuriating and cute.

"That's not the point. The point is locking him up in a cage is hurting him even more. He's not going to bite me." She reached back in my cage and petted the top of my head. "See, harmless."

"Ivy!" He rushed forward, and I lunged for him, snapping my teeth at the bars as he pulled her away from the cage. "We have no clue what his deal is. All signs point to him not having shifted in a while."

"Why would something like that happen?" She

picked up the blanket he had dropped in his haste to save her from the big bad wolf.

"A lot of reasons. He could have been kicked out of his pack, someone special to him could have died, he could be sick. No matter the reason, he has already showed signs of aggression."

He would have tried to attack any male that had his hands on his mate too. I was protecting what's mine.

"But it's perfectly fine for you to want him in your room."

I'd much prefer to be in *her* room. I could see myself curled up next to her, her hand stroking my head as I drifted off to sleep.

It had been a long time since I'd had a good sleep. Sleeping under fallen logs, abandoned buildings, and wherever else I could find didn't help with my nightmares.

A cage didn't help either.

The whine left me before I could stop it, and I sat down heavily. I just wanted to go home, if home even existed anymore.

"I wasn't going to stay in there with him." Eli took the blanket from her and put it through the bars, straightening it out in a nicely folded rectangle.

They left me then, stopping somewhere upstairs and having a hushed conversation I couldn't hear before the door shut softly.

Alone again.

I WOKE TO WARMTH. My head was resting on an outstretched arm and a hand was resting on my belly, buried in my hair. I hadn't slept so well in a long time.

Grunting, I rolled onto my belly to find the man from the night before asleep on his side, his head resting on the same arm I'd just been on.

Confusion washed over me at the pain I suddenly felt in my chest. He said I was dangerous, yet he'd slept by my side?

He looked peaceful as he slept, his long eyelashes brushing his tanned cheeks. I couldn't recall the color of his eyes—I hadn't really been paying attention the night before—but I imagined they were a dark brown.

Why did it matter?

Getting to my feet, I tried to not move too fast. My mouth was incredibly dry, and I needed water. The plate was still on the floor with water on it, so I lapped that up, but it was quickly gone.

Damn. The bottle was right out of reach of my muzzle. Whoever designed the bars of this cage deserved an award because it was hard as a wolf to sink my teeth into anything.

A soft snore came from the man—I think his name was Eli—and I knew I couldn't wake him. I could just shift for a second, grab the water, then be back in no time.

Yeah. I could do that. My wolf was thirsty enough to let me out.

I didn't anticipate how painful shifting would be after not having done it in a while. A garbled cry fell from my lips, and my entire body felt like it had been stuck with a million needles. I collapsed onto the ground, unable to hold my weight with my shaky, malnourished limbs.

Shift back, you idiot.

I tried, but my body was not having it, so instead I curled into a ball.

"Oh shit." Eli was awake and jumped to his feet, grabbing the blanket from the ground. "Welcome back."

He put the blanket over my body, and I pulled it tightly around me. I was a fucking mess and probably looked like the guy at the end of *Castaway*. I felt like I had been stranded on an island for years.

"I need to check with my alpha to see if we can free you. What's your name?" He reached outside the cage and grabbed his cellphone.

My mouth was so dry that my name got part way stuck in my throat. "Xander." Damn it. I tried to say Alexander again, but nothing but air came out.

"Xander, we're going to take care of you, okay?" His voice was so soothing that my eyes closed. I'd just woken up, but shifting took everything out of me.

The last thing I remembered before passing out is looking up at Eli's worried brown eyes.

CHAPTER TWENTY-FOUR

Eli

Xander was in bad shape, and Cole wasn't answering my texts. It was barely six in the morning, and I didn't want to wake him. Making an executive decision to go with my gut, I unlocked the chains and opened the cage door.

Rolling Xander onto his back, I wrapped the blanket around him and then scooped him up. I wasn't going to leave him lying on a cold floor when he looked like he'd seen better days.

I carefully climbed the stairs and went to my room, shutting and locking the door behind me. Really, what the guy needed was an hour-long shower, a haircut, and a shave, but I wasn't about to wake him. I could wash my sheets later.

After putting him on the bed, I pulled another

blanket over him. He rolled over on his side, grabbed one of my pillows, and hugged it to his chest.

Frowning at the feeling in my chest over the sight of him cuddled up to my pillow in my bed, I went to my computer and powered it on. Now that I had a name, I could see if he was in the database for missing wolves. The name Xander wasn't a common one, so it should be easy enough.

Zero matches found. I tried spelling it several ways before opening the advanced search. I had little to go on besides he was about six feet tall, with brown hair and green eyes. Ten results came back, and I scrolled through the list, none of them looking even close to the wolf in my bed.

I shut my laptop and went into my bathroom to shower and change before heading to the kitchen to start breakfast. Cole was at the kitchen table staring at his phone and didn't look up when I walked in.

"Good morning." I grabbed my coffee cup and poured myself some. "Ivy still sleeping?"

"Probably." He took a long drink of his coffee and watched me as I got sausage and eggs out of the refrigerator. "You moved him to your room?"

"You didn't text me back. I decided not to leave a man that was suffering lying on a concrete floor." I opened the package of sausages and put them in a pan to cook.

"And if he shifts in your bedroom?" Cole put his phone down and gave me the look that told me he wasn't happy—two lines between his eyes and a frown.

"I shut the door. If he shifts and tears it up, well, I've

been meaning to redecorate." I placed six pieces of sourdough bread on a baking sheet and put them in the oven. "It was better me than Ivy. You know if she would have gone down there this morning and seen he was human, she would have let him out." I wasn't about to tell him I spent the night in there.

"I don't need you to become reckless. I have enough on my plate at the moment." He ran a hand over his face. "Dante wants to have a meeting to discuss quarantining all new wolves for a week before allowing them to mingle with the pack. And on top of that, he wants us to run a full physical, including blood work, on Ivy."

"I don't agree with locking new wolves away somewhere. How is that a good measure of how they'll behave? Running her blood through our system wouldn't be a bad idea. We might find out who her parents are." I flipped the sausages over and got busy cracking eggs in a bowl. "Want me to talk to her about it?"

"No. I will." He stood and stretched. "Damn, the treehouse really did a number on my back."

I sighed. The treehouse. I could not get the images out of my head and had jacked off twice since then thinking about it. "You're okay with me and Ivy?"

"My wolf was a little standoffish at first, but after the treehouse..." He pulled plates out of the cupboard.

"And what we did was fine?" We were close, but I wasn't sure if he wanted us to be *that* close.

"I was so focused on her, it was like you were an extension of her body." He shrugged. "If we're going to do this, things are going to touch."

"I'd hardly call my ball sack an extension of her." I laughed and sprinkled cheese on top of the eggs that just finished cooking.

"Did I just walk in on a conversation I shouldn't have?" Ivy shuffled across the kitchen and straight to the coffee. "Why do you two get up so damn early when you don't have to?"

"Wouldn't you normally get up early on a weekday?" Cole's amusement was nice to see. He had been far too grumpy lately. It was a nice change.

"But if I don't have anywhere to be, why get up?" She squeezed my ass as she walked past me, and I grinned. I loved when she touched me.

Love.

My grin fell, and I turned to the oven to check that the bread wasn't burning. Was I really already having feelings that deep for her? The thought of her leaving had made my chest hurt the day before, so it was possible I was well on my way. It was soon, though. Wasn't it?

Who put a timeline on love anyway? Everyone was different. Some fell hard and fast, while others took the long winding path.

"I have pack stuff to do, as usual." Cole leaned over once Ivy sat and kissed her.

"Mm... pack stuff? That's literally all you guys do is run a pack? Seems like with less than four hundred it would be a part-time gig. How do you get your money? I mean, look at this place." She gestured around the kitchen. "Do you grow weed in that greenhouse of yours?"

I threw my head back and laughed. It wasn't a bad idea, but marijuana really messed us up. "No. I don't grow weed out there. You should go out there and look around today."

"So it's not weed." She snapped her fingers. "I know. You dirty dogs. You have a best friends butt stuff Only Fans, don't you?"

"We do not have an Only Fans." Cole chuckled and a grin spread across his face. "Do you want us to start one?"

Ivy nearly choked on her coffee. "You can do one for your feet. Save any butt stuff action for my eyes only."

"There will be no butt action with me and Cole." I made four plates and carried three of them to the table. One was for Xander whenever he woke up again. "I help manage tech for the pack."

"A lot of the pack have regular jobs nearby or run their own small businesses from home. I inherited most of my money, but I also worked until about four years ago when my father stepped down as alpha." What he didn't tell her was the alpha of the Arbor pack before it split in two was best friends with his father and left him every cent since he had no family. "We are a pretty wealthy pack thanks to my father's investments of our assets too."

"And where is your father?" She leaned over her steaming plate and inhaled. I had never known anything other than having a good sense of smell. My inner scientist wanted to investigate why she had only just now shifted, but I needed to approach it with caution so I wouldn't overwhelm her.

"Him, my mom, and Eli's dad have been traveling around to the other packs for over a year." He took a bite of his toast and gave me a nod in appreciation. "A lot of older pack members like to travel around together. We usually get our fair share of visitors in the fall."

Ivy turned her attention to me after a couple bites of food. "Why aren't you eating yet?"

"In case you or Cole are still hungry, you can have my plate." Saying it out loud to someone was ridiculous, but it was that way for a reason.

An omega's duty was to take care of the pack, and that meant making sure those that did the protecting were taken care of first. My wolf sometimes pushed back when Sara was around because she reminded him he could easily best her, but he had become used to being last.

"And what happens if you eat all your food and then the other wolves are still hungry?" She sure had a ton of questions.

"Ivy... this is just the way it is. He doesn't have to act like this when it's just us, but he does anyway." Cole shrugged and went back to eating his food.

"They can run me out of the pack." At least, that's what was rumored to happen. The humans in us would probably abhor the idea, but our wolves ran by a different code that we couldn't always control.

Ivy put her fork down. "Well then, I'm not going to eat anymore until you catch up."

Cole grumbled and continued eating, watching me closely. He was probably wondering why he hadn't thought of that. I couldn't have my mate go hungry, so I picked up my fork and dug in, Ivy following my lead. It was nice to eat right along with people for once.

"Since I'm not doing anything today, I was thinking I could borrow a car and go shopping," Ivy said, hope in her voice as she put down her fork.

"Absolutely not." Cole stood and grabbed all of our plates. Dishes were one thing I didn't protest him doing.

"Why not? I won't go to Arbor Falls. You really can't think I'm going to sit around here and do nothing day after day." She pulled her phone out of her pocket. "You know what? I'll just call an Uber."

Cole set the plates down with a clang and plucked the phone from her hands. I sucked in a breath, already sensing the tension increasing in the room. Ivy was fire and Cole was ice.

"Maybe I can-"

"It's not safe. Or did you forget that less than a week ago someone tried to kill me? A threat to me is a threat to the entire pack, which now includes you." I hoped Cole didn't snap her phone in half with the way he was gripping it. He was pretty level-headed, but with Ivy, he forgot she wasn't one that could be controlled with an iron fist.

"Maybe they wouldn't have tried to kill us if you weren't such a jerk," she muttered.

Oh, shit.

"What was that?" Cole looked ready to bend her

over his lap and give her a spanking. My dick twitched at the thought.

Ivy stood and pushed in her chair. "I'm going to go check on our wolf friend. Let me have my phone."

"You won't. He shifted and is asleep in Eli's room." Cole put her phone in her hand, picked up the dishes, and went to put them in the sink. "You know what. You can go shopping. Sara and Manny can go with you. It will be safer shopping than here with an unhinged male."

"I'm a grown ass woman. You really think werewolf assassins are going to come for me during the day with a bunch of people around?" She threw her hands up. "I don't need chaperones."

"You never know. You never expected to shift into a wolf, did you?" Cole walked into the living room and opened a cabinet in the entertainment center where he kept a small safe. He entered his code, grabbed some money, then handed it to Ivy.

She counted it. "You sure do like throwing money at me, Cole Delaney. One might start to think I'm your bitch." She laughed. "That's probably a little too accurate."

~

ONCE IVY WAS GONE, Cole left to meet with the betas, and I went to check on Xander. I hadn't told Cole about finding out his name or that I hadn't found him in the database. The database was fairly recent and not all packs wanted to put their information online.

There was the possibility that Xander had left his pack on his own or they had kicked him out. I refused to think it could be a trap to take over our pack, something more nefarious, like he had lost his mind and was going to go on a killing spree.

Opening the door to my bedroom, I found him in the same place I'd left him. I turned and carefully shut the door, keeping the doorknob turned, trying not to make any sounds as the door shut.

Suddenly, I was shoved against the door, heat at my back as a forearm came to press against the back of my neck. "Who the fuck are you and where am I?" His rough voice washed over me like a warm blanket, and I shivered.

"Eli. You showed up in East Arbor territory... in California." He pressed harder into me, and I whimpered, despite trying to hold it in. "I'm not going to hurt you."

"Where are the others?" He spoke fast and his voice cracked.

"The others?" I didn't know who he was referring to, but with him agitated and scared, I wasn't about to tell him where Cole and Ivy were.

"Liam, Cal, and Austin? Are they dead?" He increased the pressure of his arm. "If you killed them..."

"I don't know who those people are. You showed up here alone." Didn't he remember anything from when he woke up or the day before?

"Alone?" He spun me around and his forearm pushed against my throat. "Tell me where you have them."

Nothing came out when I opened my mouth to speak. He was pressing against my throat, and I had a hard time getting air. His green eyes were troubled, but the rest of his face had a cold, detached expression. It was really off putting with the dirt smears and scruffy beard.

I wrapped my hands around his forearm and pulled down, getting him to loosen the pressure so I could speak. "I don't know where they are," I choked out as I tried to catch my breath.

He stumbled back and put his head in his hands, fisting his overgrown, tangled hair. "Where is she?"

He was coming back toward me, but I wasn't about to move and let him out of the room, so I did the only thing I could think of, I took his cheeks in my hands. "Listen to me. You came here alone and had probably been trapped in your wolf for a while, judging by your behavior. No one is going to hurt you, but you need to calm down and tell me what happened so I can help you."

"Ivy." His eyes darkened as they dilated, causing my heart to thud hard enough he could probably hear it. "Where's Ivy?"

"Ivy? She went shopping." Why the hell was he asking for Ivy? Even if she was around, I wasn't about to tell him that. Maybe Cole had been right about keeping him locked in the basement, and I wasn't just saying that because he was asking about my mate.

"We have to find her before they get her!" He jerked away from me and reached for the doorknob. "Move out of my way."

"No." I calculated how long it would take me to grab a tranquilizer from my nightstand and get to him with it. They were similar to an EpiPen, and we kept them everywhere just in case. "Why don't you take a shower and I'll get you a plate of food. By the time you've cleaned up, Cole should be back."

Wrong. Thing. To. Say.

He pushed me back against the door again and got way too close for comfort given his deranged state of mind. For some unknown reason, I had felt moved to cuddle up against his wolf in the basement, but he had been harmless while sleeping.

"Cole wanted me locked up. He locked her up!" His voice cracked, and he clenched his jaw so hard that it made my jaw hurt.

What the hell was he talking about? "Only you were locked up. Just you." I felt like a broken record.

His chest was heaving. "I need to see her."

I knew that trauma could cause neurological issues, but had never witnessed it for myself. Sighing, I stood there as he growled and glared, waiting for my answer. I didn't understand why he hadn't just knocked me out of the way to get out. Maybe he did have a tendril of sanity left.

He backed up again and looked around the room. It only took him a split second to make a mad dash to the window, rip the shutters off, and go for the lock.

Darting after him, I wrapped my arms around his waist in a bear hug, and with all my strength, tackled him onto the bed. I took a knee to the groin and an elbow to my ribs before he finally exhausted himself.

The most awful sound I'd ever heard came from him, and then he was clinging to the front of my shirt with his fists, his head buried in the crook of my neck. I froze for a second before my arms went around him and gently stroked his back.

"It's going to be okay." His hot tears hit my neck, and my heart hurt for him. "Shh. You're safe now."

"I can't even protect myself and my pack, how am I going to protect her?" I could barely understand him through his tears.

Male wolves rarely showed their emotions so openly, and it made *me* want to cry too. What had happened to this wolf to hurt him so irrevocably, and how could I help fix it?

CHAPTER TWENTY-FIVE

Ivy

Shopping with Sara and Manny was better than not shopping at all. Would I have preferred to go shopping alone? Yes. Sara and Manny were going to make it that much more difficult to do what I had wanted to come to the city to do.

Putting my chin on my fist, I stared out the window of Manny's truck, trying to figure out a new plan. I was supposed to meet with Charles Scott, a social worker who had been in my dad's contacts and who had been in charge of my adoption.

"You're awfully quiet." Sara turned her head to look at me from the front seat. "I thought you wanted to get out."

Shit. I needed to pretend better so they didn't grow

suspicious. "I am. Just didn't expect to have babysitters is all."

Manny laughed. "I'm surprised he let you come. He must really be worried about the new wolf being at the house."

"He's a person, not just a wolf." I met his eyes in the rearview mirror. "How many times has Cole been locked in his basement?"

Manny went back to watching the highway, his shoulders stiff. "He hasn't."

"Well, maybe he needs to be so he can see what it's like." I crossed my arms over my chest. "It's not pleasant to wake up confused in a fucking cage."

"I agree with that. But..." Sara sighed. "When I was fifteen, my mom and I got in a car accident—that's how I lost my leg—and she lost her life. Eli didn't take it well."

A pang went through my chest at the thought of Eli suffering. "He was locked up?"

She nodded. "For about a week. I wasn't there to witness it, but Cole said Eli's wolf took over. He would have run off if they hadn't locked him up."

"What does that accomplish? Letting your wolf take over?" Maybe it was the same thing for me, except opposite.

"Makes the emotional pain easier to deal with. But with me, I couldn't shift to my wolf for the longest time. There's three different types of trauma with us. The wolf only, the human only, or a combination. An imbalance of that can make one overpower the other."

"What kind of trauma did I experience to go

twenty-six years without shifting?" I frowned out the window as Manny pulled off the highway and drove into the city.

It wasn't a city like Los Angeles or New York, but a hundred thousand people, when you were used to less than ten thousand, was a big difference. There was one mall, and that was where we were going.

"Sometimes people haven't been able to shift to their wolves after a traumatic event happened that really shook their wolf up. It took me three years. You were abandoned, so maybe that has something to do with it." Sara had a point, but babies also didn't have memories or understand things, so I didn't see how that could be it.

"Does the brain even recognize those kinds of things so soon after being born?"

Sara shrugged. "I sometimes think I remember what it feels like to be in the womb."

Manny laughed, and Sara punched his arm as he pulled into a parking structure. "Ow, that really fucking hurt."

For being a beta, Manny wasn't that tough.

∽

I PUT on a good show of being interested in shopping. Manny was getting bored and instead of waiting inside the stores while Sara and I tried clothes on, he waited just outside with his eyes glued to his phone.

"Sara, I'm done. I'll be right outside, okay?" I had pretended to try on clothes for an adequate amount of time. From the other three stores we'd been in, she took twice as long as me. Ample time for an escape.

"Sounds good." She grunted, and I knew she was in the middle of trying on some jeans I'd talked her into trying.

I'd already requested an Uber and had five minutes to get outside.

Leaving the dressing room, I took my items to the front counter where one employee was working on folding shirts. "Excuse me, my friend Sara would like a size ten in every color in that style of jean you have. She really likes that one pair."

"I'm so glad she liked them! I'll get those for her right now. Are you ready to check out? I can call someone up here to ring you up." It was a smaller shop, and another woman was near the front of the store putting away merchandise.

"Oh, no. I'm still going to browse a bit and wait for my friend."

After a quick glance to the front of the store to ensure Manny wasn't looking, I hurried to the entry where there was a sign that said, "Employees Only." As soon as I was in the small hallway that led to the back of the store, I ran for the exit at the back.

Time was of the essence. They wouldn't look at the tracking on my phone right away, so I had time to get my Uber and be on my way.

Exiting the back of the store, I was in a long hallway with doors to a lot of other shops. I rushed down the hall to the door that would spit me out near the bathrooms.

The thing was, I probably could have told Cole about the contact I'd found the day before, but this was personal and I didn't need someone right next to me to meet with a social worker.

I headed into the mall and then walked out the main entrance where a small blue SUV waited for me. I slid into the backseat and the driver took off to the coffee shop I agreed to meet the man at.

We were just about to the destination when my phone vibrated with a text message from Sara. *"Where are you?"*

"In the bathroom. There's a line. Meet you guys outside the store?"

As soon as I texted, I silenced the phone and slipped it into the back seat pocket as we pulled into the parking lot. I opened my wallet and took out two hundred dollars of the money Cole had given me. "I have an odd request if you're up for two hundred dollars."

The driver, who looked to be an upstanding middle-aged citizen, raised his eyebrow and turned to look at me as he stopped the car. "Is it legal?"

Laughing, I flashed him the money. "Yes. I need you to drive back to the mall, park, and then come back to get me in about an hour."

"Why the mall? I can just wait here."

"Do you want two hundred dollars or not?" My other option was to just abandon my phone and hope I could get it back later.

"You kids these days. Sure, I'll do it since it's not that

far." He took the money, and I just hoped he did actually come back.

I slid out of the backseat and walked inside the coffee shop. My hands were shaking slightly as I looked around for Charles. I had done some internet stalking and found his picture on social media.

Spotting him, my pulse raced as I walked to the table he was at. "Charles? I'm Ivy."

He stood and shook my hand before we sat down. "It's wonderful to meet you. It's not often us social workers get to see the children we help find homes for once they're grown."

He seemed nice enough, and I relaxed back into my chair. I had a ton of questions for him which couldn't be asked when I'd called him the day before.

"I'm so sorry about your parents." He gave me a sympathetic smile. "Now, what questions can I answer for you?"

"Do you know who my parents are?" I assumed Child Protective Services had exhausted all efforts to locate them.

"No one came forward and there were no hospitals or doctors within driving distance that had seen a postpartum woman. We immediately placed you with a foster family while we waited the requisite amount of time to find a home for you."

I hadn't even considered that. "Were my parents my foster parents too?"

"No. Well, not at first." He ran a hand through his salt and pepper colored hair. "You had a good life?"

"Yes. My parents were the best." Using the word

were made tears well up in my eyes. "I wish they would have told me about being adopted, but maybe they had their reasons."

He shifted in his seat. "Your adoption was a bit atypical."

My breath got caught in my throat. Did he know? "What do you mean by that?"

"About a week after you were found, a man came to see me." He looked around the coffee shop like someone was going to suddenly appear. "You have to understand, I was young, had a ton of student loan debt, a newborn of my own..."

Unease filled me, and I clasped my hands tightly in my lap. "What..." I gulped. "What does that have to do with anything?"

"I was assigned to your case and working with adoption agencies to find a permanent placement for you. The man came in and offered me a large sum of money to make sure you ended up far away from here."

What. The. Fuck.

I cleared my throat of the ball of nervousness that had lodged there. "Was it my father?"

He shook his head quickly. "No, I don't think he was. He said he was a friend of your father's but couldn't give me any other information. He also wanted me to keep him updated of where you ended up."

"What was his name?" I was pretty sure my heart had stopped beating.

"He didn't give me a name, and he always came to find me and paid me in cash." He ran a hand over his face. "I found your parents a few weeks later, and once your adoption was official, he stopped showing up."

"Do you remember anything about him?" Arbor Falls was only so big, and hope welled in my chest. I was that much closer to finding out who my birth parents were.

"He was a mean-looking man, a biker. Had blonde hair and green eyes. Oh, and he had a scar on his cheek like someone had sliced him open."

That sounded like Silas, but it couldn't have been Silas since he was Cole's age and I didn't remember a scar on his cheek. Was I related to Silas? I inwardly cringed at the thought.

"And you haven't heard from this man since all those years ago?" I found it hard to believe someone concerned enough to pay for me to go far away would stop asking for updates.

"Not once." He let out a relieved sigh. "You aren't mad?"

Mad? No. Confused? Yes. "How much did he give you?"

"Oh, well..." He turned bright red and looked down at his hands. "Five hundred thousand."

My eyes nearly popped out of my skull. "And that didn't seem fishy to you at all?"

"It did, but it's not like I could have said no. Like I said, he did not look like someone to mess with, and I had a wife and baby to worry about. It seemed harmless to have you adopted far away. I figured it was because it would have been too hard on your um..."

"Real parents?"

"Yeah." He looked at his watch. "I should probably get going. I'm sorry I couldn't be more help. Feel free to call me if you have more questions."

He left me sitting there, digesting the information he'd given me. Arbor Falls was my home and someone had something to do with me moving far away. The question was why?

Waiting outside for the Uber driver that was hopefully going to return, I was more upset than I'd ever been about being adopted. What had been so wrong with me or my parents that someone would pay half a million dollars never to see me again?

Was it because I looked different? Who were my parents and why hadn't they wanted me? There was one person who probably knew that answer, and there was no way in hell Cole was going to let me contact him.

The Uber driver pulled into the parking lot, and I opened the back door. "Any problems?"

"There were some angry-looking people looking around the parking lot. They didn't bother me, but they looked around my vehicle." He turned to look at me. "What kind of trouble are you in?"

I pulled my phone out of the back seat pocket and quickly glanced around. "I'll be fine. I think I'll walk. Thanks!"

He started to say something, but I slammed the door shut and walked across the parking lot, I was probably going to be easy to spot with my damn hair. I should have thought to wear a hat.

Looking at my phone, I sighed. I had missed calls

and messages from Cole, Sara, and Eli. I was a grown ass woman, and they made me feel like I was about to get grounded.

I probably was.

There was a park nearby I walked to and sat on a swing, waiting for them to find me. I read through Sara's messages, which went from being annoyed, to pissed off, to amused. Then there were Cole's.

Cole: *Where the fuck are you? Sara called me and said you disappeared.*

Cole: *Answer your phone, Ivy.*

Cole: *You better hope I don't find you first.*

I bit my lip and looked around. So far, so good. The park was empty since it was midweek and the middle of the day.

Me: *Yeah? What are you going to do to me, Alpha?*

I slid my phone into my purse and pushed off the ground. I hadn't been on a swing in forever, and it was liberating to have the wind rush through my hair and blood rushing through my body as I went higher and higher.

Oh, geez. Was this a canine thing? Now I understood why I enjoyed swings so much growing up.

The rush soon gave way to an intense feeling of loss. Loss of my parents, loss of whatever life I might have had with people like me, loss of my freedom.

My feet dragged on the bark under the swing and I came to a stop, leaning forward with my face in my hands. I had just started living my life in a career I loved, and now it was being ripped away from me.

Cole's scent was the first thing that made me aware

that I was no longer alone in my pity party. I really wasn't in the mood to deal with him and his overbearing personality.

"Ivy." The swing next to me squeaked as he sat down. "What the hell were you thinking?"

With a sigh, I dropped my hands and stared off at the slide that had seen better days. "I guess I wasn't." I let the tears drip freely down my face. "Get your berating over with and take me back to my prison."

"It's not a prison." His voice has softened.

"Sure feels like it. I can't go anywhere, have a tracker on my phone, have to worry about being locked up in solitary confinement. It's a prison." One I hadn't exactly fought that hard against.

He tensed, and his knuckles turned white on the chains of the swing. "You don't understand how dangerous it is for us." He sounded like a broken record. Did he think I didn't know that? That didn't mean I had to be locked away. "What if you would have shifted during your little adventure?"

I jumped off the swing and turned to glare at him. "What if I would have when I didn't live here?" My voice rose, and I shut my eyes to calm myself down before I proved him right and shifted. "It wasn't too dangerous for someone to leave me in a fucking ivy bush. Why is that, Cole? What's so bad about this place... or about me, to send me away like I didn't even matter?"

The chains on the swing clinked together as Cole stood, putting his hands on my arms. "You do matter."

I put my forehead against his chest. "They didn't want me."

"Hey, look at me." He pulled back and tilted my chin up. "They're idiots, whoever they are. You're a strong, independent woman who takes no shit and knows what she wants. If they could see you now, they'd probably regret letting you go."

He was right, but all these feelings of rejection were growing intense. I needed answers, not just for myself, but for the wolf part of me.

"I'm sorry for running off." I snorted back a laugh. "Jesus, maybe I should start calling you daddy since I feel you're going to punish me."

"That can be arranged, although I prefer hearing you scream Cole." He kissed the top of my head. "I wish you'd trust me a little more. I'm trying to keep you safe."

It was hard to trust when I barely knew him. Yes, there was an intense connection between us that made me want to simultaneously rip off his head and rip off his clothes, but trusting someone so easily was difficult.

I leaned in as his hand stroked my cheek. "I'm trying."

Sometimes trying had to be good enough.

CHAPTER TWENTY-SIX

Cole

It was a quiet drive home, and I could tell Ivy was keeping something from me. I hadn't exactly asked her what she'd been up to in the hour she'd been MIA, but I had a feeling it was why she was in the state she was in at the park.

I'd been furious when I'd gotten the call from Sara that she'd run off. It couldn't have come at a worse time either. I'd been ensuring my betas and other high-ranking heads of families that there was nothing to worry about with Ivy.

While I hadn't told them why I'd left in a hurry, I was sure Manny had already filled Dante in since he reported directly to him. Things might be bad when we got back to the house. I was the alpha, but if enough betas and stronger wolves banded together, I wouldn't be able to stop them.

"Are you going to eventually tell me what you were up to?" I asked as I pulled off the highway and drove down the road to my house.

"Yes, but I'm still processing it." She put her hand over mine that was resting on the center console. "It's going to make you angry."

Flipping my hand over, I laced our fingers together. "How about you give me a blow job and then tell me?"

She finally cracked a smile and brought our hands to her lips, kissing my knuckles. "Is that what it takes to make everything right? A blow job?"

"Pretty simple, isn't it?" I had to pull my hand away to back into the driveway and she snorted. "Tell me what makes everything all right for you?"

She unhooked her seatbelt once we parked. "Ice cream, wine, or chocolate."

We got out of the truck, and I took her hand again as we walked to the front door. "I have all three."

"You've been holding out on me, Delaney." She bumped her shoulder into mine. "Everyone knows the first rule of having a girlfriend is to always keep them supplied with the good stuff."

"Girlfriend. I think I like the sound of that." Outside of being mates, we hadn't put a definition on what we were. I was happy she was on the same page as me, and my wolf was satisfied, for now.

We didn't even get all the way in the house when a growl came from the couch and a man flew across the room, knocking me into the wall. I twisted away and charged him, knocking him back and away from Ivy.

"Stop it!" Eli was already trying to separate us, but there was no way I was letting this asshole, who I only assumed was the stray wolf, get away with attacking me in my house.

He swung at me and I ducked, coming up with an uppercut that sent his head flying back and caused blood to drip from his mouth. His eyes were those of his wolf's and I knew we were in dangerous territory if I didn't get him to submit.

Eli fumbled in a drawer, pulling out a tranquilizer pen and popping the cap off. "Here." He tried handing it to me, and I shook my head.

I needed to put this guy in his place and then lock him back in the basement. Maybe Dante wasn't completely out of his mind when he suggested a one-week quarantine to ensure this kind of thing didn't happen.

"Mine." His lip pulled back off his teeth to reveal his canines, and he lunged for me again.

I sidestepped at the last second, and he ran headfirst into the wall, falling backward onto his ass with a whimper of pain.

"Dante, you're needed in the house." I didn't want to seek his help, but if I couldn't get this guy to submit, I'd need help getting him into the basement. I wouldn't put Eli and Ivy in danger.

Ivy tried to move past me, and I moved my body in front of hers. "Maybe you should wait outside. This might get ugly. I don't want you to get hurt."

Dante came in the backdoor and came straight for us just as the guy pulled himself up and made another move for me. Ivy darted past me and stopped Dante with a shove to his chest.

"Stay back! This has nothing to do with you." Her voice was distorted by what I could only guess were her canines.

In my distraction, I was mowed to the ground, my head bouncing on the hardwood floor and my vision spotting with black dots. He grabbed me by the throat but just as suddenly let go, listing to the side and falling in a heap with Eli standing over him, panting. He'd used the tranquilizer.

"Are you okay?" Eli dropped the injector and came to me, helping me sit up. "There's no blood. How's your vision? That was a really hard hit."

I blinked hard a few times and my eyes blurred. "Eh, I'll be fine." I rubbed at them, hoping that would help. Ivy and Dante were in a stare down with growls coming from both of them. It surprised me they hadn't shifted.

"Enough!" I let Eli help me to my feet and grimaced as I took a few steps toward them. "Back off her, Dante."

"Un-fucking-believable! She comes after me twice now and you tell *me* to back off? Must be some really good pussy to make you change allegiance after less than a week." He backed away from Ivy and faced me. "How do we know she's not going to go rabid like this fucker over on the floor?"

Despite feeling woozy, I met him face to face, our

toes nearly touching and his hot breath fanning across my face. "Watch your mouth, Beta, or next time her wolf challenges you, I'll let her rip you to shreds." My voice was deadly and Dante's eyes went wide before he stepped back and dropped his gaze. "Do you understand me?"

"Yes, Alpha," Dante grumbled his response, and I stepped closer again and let my wolf come to the surface. "Yes, Alpha."

"Get out of my sight. We can handle this from here." I gave him my back and he let out a strangled whimper he tried to hold back before I heard his footsteps retreating to the back door.

"Let's get him to the basement," I directed.

"No." Ivy moved in front of me and stood over the man. "He'll sleep in my room."

I was taken aback by the authoritative tone in her voice, and my wolf bristled. "He's dangerous. Did you not see that or were you too busy challenging my beta, yet again?"

"Maybe you need better betas." She squatted down next to the man and smoothed a hand across his forehead. "Eli, will you help me?"

Eli looked from me back to her. "Xander's been through a lot. We can't just lock him back up. I managed to get him to shower, and I shaved his hair and his mountain man beard he had going on."

"He was on the couch. You should have waited for me to get here." I didn't take my eyes off Ivy, who was stroking the guy's cheek now. "What the hell are you doing, Ivy?"

"I think... he's my mate." She shook her head. "Unbelievable."

Eli cleared his throat. "It makes sense now why he kept asking about you. I thought he was just confused."

"I need to go for a run." My wolf was ready to come out and rip out Xander's throat. I didn't want to share with some stranger that limped in looking like he'd been tramping around in the forest for months on end.

I had just made it past the island in the kitchen, heading to the door, when Ivy grabbed my arm. "Cole, wait."

"What?" Stopping, I shrugged off her hand and pulled my shirt over my head. Her eyes went to my chest. "I need a few minutes."

Eli had disappeared with Xander, and I narrowed my eyes. What the fuck was going on in my own house? I didn't even have control over my own damn omega.

"Let's talk about this. I know three mates isn't an ideal situation, but I can't help it. We should be asking why I have three mates, not getting upset about it." She shrugged as if it was no big deal, and that was the only reason I needed to get away.

"I need a few minutes so I don't lash out at you." Her face fell, and I took a step closer to her. "You drive me fucking nuts with your back talking and ability to push my buttons… and then you look at me with these eyes…" I swiped a finger across the soft skin under her eye. "Seduce me with these curves." I slowly ran my hand down her side and squeezed her hip. "Taunt me with these lips."

Me needing a breather suddenly went out the window, and I gently brushed my lips against hers, and she groaned. I loved the way she trembled against me, and I slid my hand to her lower back, pulling her flush against me and deepening the kiss.

I smoothed my hands over her ass before lifting her onto the island, her legs wrapping around me. I had never wanted a woman as bad as I wanted Ivy in that moment, especially when she shivered as my lips trailed down her neck and placed the lightest kisses on her cleavage. Thank the moon for low cut shirts.

Just as my fingers were making their way under her shirt, Sara walked into the kitchen. I hadn't even heard or smelled her enter the damn house.

"Uh, this is awkward as fuck. Remind me not to eat there." She just waltzed right in and went to the refrigerator, where she started pulling out what looked to be the makings of a sandwich.

"You need to lock your doors, Cole." Ivy ran her fingers through my hair as she buried her face in my neck and let out a defeated and annoyed groan.

"I have a key." Sara casually made a sandwich with us still on the counter, obviously waiting for her to leave. "By the way, great job escaping today. I applaud your efforts. Way to stick it to the man." She took a bite out of her sandwich and leaned against the counter. "I had a look at the locator data and then hacked into the security cameras at the coffee shop."

Ivy's face fell, and she slid off the counter. "Sara-"

"You should tell him." She pointed her sandwich at me and then walked out of the kitchen humming to herself, leaving the mustard and turkey out for someone else to put away.

"Tell me what?" My need to run was strong, and I clenched my fists.

"I'll tell you tonight, all right?" She looked down at her feet.

My nostrils flared with each breath I took, and I went to the door, unbuttoning my pants and kicking off my shoes as I went.

"Cole-"

My body jolted forward as soon as the sliding door was open far enough, and I ran for the trees.

~

My muscles pulsated as I ran through the forest. Too much had happened, and I needed a moment to breathe away from it all. Being alpha wasn't my first choice in life, but my pack had needed a strong leader and no one else was good enough. Some days were harder than others; today being one of those days.

I came to my favorite clearing where wildflowers were just budding and filled the air with their fragrant aroma. I inhaled deeply and my wolf was confused by the smell. What was that?

Putting my nose to the ground, I tried sniffing it out, but it was in the air. It was a cloying sort of smell that put my wolf on edge, but I couldn't identify it.

A loud explosion filled the silence and pain ripped through me as I fell onto my side.

I've been shot.

I tried to get back to my feet, but the pain was too much. How had a hunter gotten into our territory? Where were my betas and the patrols? I tried to open a connection to anyone to get help, but everything was cutoff.

I'm going to die.

CHAPTER TWENTY-SEVEN

Ivy

We went through the gate of the Southern Shelf, guns out and ready to fire. Sara preferred a shotgun, me a semi-automatic rifle. As we walked across the icy snow, our boots crunched. On the right was Gateway Harbor, where we could see a marauder or some other villain patrolling.

Sara was the guns blazing type, while I preferred a slower and more stealth approach. Good thing I chose the character that had amazing healing capabilities to heal her reckless ass.

"So, you just hacked into the security and listened to my whole conversation?" I ran after her as she went through the gates and a psycho ran at her. She blew him away with her shotgun while I hit the marauder.

More red dots appeared on our map, signaling we were about to be overrun by the enemy.

"The safety of the pack comes above all else. If that means invading your privacy, then that's what I'll do." She shrugged as I followed her character back through the gates. "You have close friends, right?"

"Yes." My eyes didn't move from the screen where we were about to go storming in, despite how outnumbered we were.

"And you're fiercely protective of them, right? They're your pack too." She started pressing her buttons at a fast rate as she came out of hiding and started taking down the enemy.

She was right. I was protective of my friends and always had been. That didn't mean I still wasn't a little mad that she'd watched the security footage.

"I didn't tell Cole yet."

Sara didn't respond at first. Whether it was because she just died on the game and I wasn't reviving her, or she was thinking, I'll never know.

"It's Silas's dad... the one that paid the social worker." She put down her controller and turned toward me. "He disappeared a decade ago, and that's when Silas took over for the western pack. He was younger than me, so as you can imagine, it's been rough watching that pack fall apart."

"He's not a good alpha?" I turned off the game, my eyes burning from staring at the screen for too long. I liked video games, just not what they did to my eyes.

"I think he could be, but his father didn't exactly leave the pack in a good place. They were broke, and now that I know about the half million, that's probably why." Sara stood and stretched. "I'm going to head home."

Cole hadn't returned, and I texted Eli to tell him I was concerned. He came down the hall a few minutes later, looking like he had just woken up from a nap. I raised an eyebrow as Xander came out behind him.

"I'll go look for him." Eli turned to Xander. "Are you going to be okay here with Ivy?"

Xander nodded and Eli went to the back door, leaving me alone with a wolf who had just been tranquilized because he attacked Cole.

He stared at me, not moving an inch, and I turned back toward the television. "Want to watch a movie?"

My body was attuned to his movements as he stepped forward. In the reflection on the television screen, I saw him staring down at the back of my head.

A part of me knew he wouldn't hurt me because we were mates, but that didn't stop a chill from spreading across my arms and a brief tremble escaped.

"You're cold." His voice was soft, almost a whisper, as he grabbed a crocheted blanket that was folded on a chair and came to stand in front of me.

Leaning forward, he threw it around me. I looked up at him and bit my lip, not sure what to say to this man. What if I upset him and he went crazy? Eli wouldn't have left him alone with me if he thought it was going to happen, though.

"Are you going to sit down?" I leaned back and held the controller up to point at the television. "Kind of hard to find something to watch with you standing in the way."

Instead of sitting, he laid down with his head in my lap. My heart rate sped up, and I distracted myself by quickly picking one of those small-town romance movies that were addicting.

After putting down the remote, I tried to figure out what to do with my hands and arms. Usually I hugged a pillow or kept my hands resting on my thighs, but I couldn't do that with a strange man's head in the way.

"I can move." His head started to lift, and I stopped him. He inhaled sharply before lowering back to rest his head on my thigh.

I kept my hand on his head, which was shaved short, the small hairs soft against my hand. "It's weird having a mate, isn't it?"

He grunted as I stroked his head. "You have three."

Three boyfriends was a lot to digest, and I hoped that was it because I didn't know how my vagina was going to handle more than three cocks. I snorted back a laugh and Xander rolled onto his back to look up at me.

"We're supposed to be watching the movie." Who was I kidding, I'd have to restart it because I missed the first few minutes and had no clue why the chick was crying in the airport.

"I want to look at your face." His green eyes were troubled, and his brows drew in as he stared up at me. He looked tired and like he hadn't slept in days, but was clean shaven with short hair. What I assumed were Eli's clothes, fit loosely on his body.

"Cole's been shot. Call Sara and get her to the house immediately." Eli's voice was frantic in my head and I jumped up without thinking about it, sending Xander flailing onto the floor.

"Where's my phone?" I patted my pockets and looked around frantically. "Fuck!"

With a shaking hand, Xander held out my phone, which must have fallen when I stood. "Did I do something wrong?"

"No! Cole's been shot!" I dialed Sara and yelled the same thing at her before rushing to the back door, Xander right behind me.

Time stood still as I went onto the deck and looked across the dark backyard. How could Cole have been shot? There were supposed to be patrols guarding the territory.

"This is all my fault." I jabbed my fingers through my hair and ran across the yard as Eli came into view, carrying a bloodied wolf in his arms. "What the hell happened?"

"I don't know! I followed his scent to his favorite place to think and found him like this. I couldn't pick up any other scents besides him." Eli was moving as fast as he could with a large wolf in his arms and we climbed the steps. "You called Sara, right?"

"Yes. She should-"

"Bloody hell! What happened?" Sara led the way down to the basement and opened a door I'd never even thought about. Inside looked like an operating room with four large metal tables.

Eli put him down, his entire front covered in blood.

He grabbed a pair of clippers and started shaving Cole's side.

"I think I'm going to be sick." I turned, bumping right into Xander, who was paler than a ghost with terrified eyes. "Hey, let's wait upstairs." I put my hand on his cheek and backed him out of the room.

As soon as we reached the top of the stairs, he went to Eli's room and shut himself inside. The state Cole was in had triggered him and I wanted to know why, but it would have to wait.

I paced the hall outside the door leading to the basement. If I had just told Cole what happened that morning, this never would have happened.

Looking down the steps, I could see and smell Cole's blood on the stairs. A bitter smell hit my nose along with the blood. I didn't know what it was, but my wolf didn't like it.

My feet started moving down the steps; the sounds from below were frantic. As I made my way to the door where they'd taken Cole, the scene unfolded before me.

Cole was splayed out on a metal table, his side shaved for easy access to his abdomen, which had been opened to reveal more than I wanted to see. A puddle of blood was on the floor, drops of blood occasionally falling off the side of the table to join the pool of red.

Eli glanced at me before saying something to Dante, who turned and looked at me. He nodded and then walked past me and up the stairs, shutting the door behind him. When had he come in?

"There's a tunnel from the den." Eli lifted his chin

toward a door on the opposite side of the room. "That's why we keep the basement door locked."

There were so many things I had to learn and I wanted Cole to be the one who shared those things, but he looked half-dead. Bringing my hand to my mouth, I covered a sob that spilled out.

"Hand me the staple gun." Sara's voice cut off my thoughts and my attention was back on Cole.

They packed his wound with an herb that smelled musky and floral. Eli handed her the surgical staple gun, and I watched as Eli held the incision together while Sara stapled it closed and put some kind of glue on it. She wiped the sweat off her forehead with the back of her arm and stepped back.

"He should be okay in a few days. The poison is what's going to take some time to burn off."

Poison?

I approached the table and looked down at Cole, who was still lifeless with his tongue hanging out of the side of his mouth. My eyes went to the blood covering him, Eli, Sara, and the floor. There was so much, it was a miracle he wasn't going to die.

By the time they had finished cleaning up the mess and Sara left, it was nearly midnight. My stomach growled and Eli gave me a small smile. "He's probably going to be out the rest of the night. Let's go upstairs and I'll feed you. Shit, Xander is probably starving."

"What's going on there?" I stayed in the chair I had moved from the kitchen table to sit beside the table Cole was resting on.

"What do you mean?" He washed his hands in the sink and dried them on a clean rag.

"You've been protective of him and been with him in your room." I ran my hand over Cole's snout to make sure he was still breathing. I had been checking every so often because his breaths were shallow. "Not that there's anything wrong with that."

He laughed. "It's my job to take care of injured pack members or members who might need comfort."

"Well, if there was something-"

"There's not." He frowned at me. "You're my mate."

"But if there was, it would be fine to, you know... explore that." What an awkward conversation to have with someone.

"I'll keep that in mind." He gave me a funny look and pulled a blanket from a cabinet. "You aren't going to leave his side, are you?"

"We can't move him up to his bed?"

"Not until he shifts back. Those are his own rules." Eli tucked the blanket around Cole and then pulled me to my feet, wrapping his arms around me. At some point during my frazzled mental state, he'd pulled on clothes. "He'll be okay. I found him soon enough."

"What is the poison?" I rubbed my cheek on the soft fabric of his shirt, the faint smell of Cole's blood and fabric softener mixing.

"Dante." Cole's voice popped into my head and was so faint I barely heard it.

I pushed away from Eli, I almost threw myself across him, but Eli wrapped his arms around me from behind. "What are you doing?"

"He said Dante in my head." I wanted to cry but held myself together. "But that's it."

Eli stepped around me and stroked the side of Cole's head. "Alpha, what happened? Do you know who did this?"

"Dante." His voice was a little stronger and his wolf's feet twitched how dog's often do when they have dreams. *"Dante."*

"He keeps repeating Dante." I went to the other side of the table. "Cole, what about Dante? Do you want us to get him?"

There was no response, and I headed for the door.

"Where are you going?" Eli started to follow me and I stopped him. "You stay here and I'll go find Dante."

"I know nothing about treatment for wolves. What if he needs you?" I made it to the stairs. "I'll be right back. He won't be too hard to find, right?"

Eli sighed. "Can you check on Xander too?"

I gave him a peck on the cheek. "I will."

Running up the stairs, I was hopeful that Cole would wake up soon. The fact he was asking for Dante was a good sign.

As soon as I shut the door, something slammed into my side, knocking me down the hall toward the living room. Groaning, I tried to sit up, but my side hurt too much.

"Tie her up."

Dante.

My body went through the shift faster than it ever had before. My side still hurt, but it was less painful in my wolf form. I saw the benefits to staying that way if I needed to heal.

Dante locked the door to the basement. If Eli couldn't get through, that might be a good thing because there were two other giant guys besides Dante. I vaguely recognized them from seeing them in the den the night of the meeting.

A whimper came from the other side of the couch. *Mate.* If I wasn't sure before about Xander being my mate, I was now. He was tied up in his wolf form, including a muzzle over his mouth.

I growled at the approaching men and backed up toward the front door. How I was going to get it open and get out was unclear, but I wasn't foolish enough to think I could fight off three men.

"Aw, the poor little wolf is scared," Dante taunted, something gripped in his hand that looked like an EpiPen. Shit. That was a tranquilizer. "I'm the alpha now, bitch."

It happened fast.

One second I was jumping for the door, attempting to send a warning to Cole and Eli to run, and the next, heat exploded across my back and then numbness.

My body hit the floor and my eyes had a difficult time adjusting to see straight. The outlines of three figures stood over me. One squatted down, slipping something over my mouth.

"Such a shame we had to end on these terms."

I managed a growl, and he threw his head back and laughed. That was the last sound I heard before passing out.

CHAPTER TWENTY-EIGHT

Eli

How I got so lucky to have Ivy as a mate was beyond my comprehension. I felt unworthy of her, and not just because I was an omega. She had opened her heart to us when she could have easily shut us out.

I sat down in the chair Ivy had vacated and slouched, my arms crossed. How did someone manage to get far enough into our territory without being detected? Not only that, but ambush Cole and nearly kill him?

Dante was in charge of ensuring our perimeter was secure with patrols and checking the fencing. Maybe there was a downed section of fence that needed repair.

I'd have to see if Xander remembered how he got

here. If he would even talk to me. As it was, he'd said only a few things, and I hadn't even attempted to coax any information from him about what had happened to him.

Ivy was crazy if she thought there was something between him and I. Why couldn't two men seek comfort? Caring for him was part of my job as an omega, just as sitting in the chair next to Cole was.

I covered my face with one hand. Jesus. I definitely wasn't moved to cuddle up next to Cole, or stroke his hair while he nuzzled my neck.

Granted, Xander had been a mess for a while, rambling incoherently. He'd needed contact with another wolf to ease him. But if Cole woke up and needed that level of comfort... I wouldn't snuggle up to him.

But Xander? I barely knew him yet... No. It was nothing.

A thud came from upstairs, snapping me out of my confusion.

"Run!" Ivy's voice screamed in my head.

What the hell? I jumped up, and as I was about to go find out what the hell was going on upstairs, Cole shifted back.

He let out a groan and reached for me. "No."

"Alpha! You need to shift back, you aren't healed!" I took his outstretched hand, and he squeezed it so hard. I was surprised he had the strength.

"Dante... shot me," he bit out through clenched teeth. His eyes were clenched shut in pain. "He's alpha now."

"What?" I nearly shrieked. "Cole?" I slapped his cheek lightly when he seemed to pass out again. "What do I do?"

Cole's eyelids cracked open a sliver. The look in his eyes made my heart falter. "Run. Ivy said... run."

He shifted back, his wolf's body going limp on the table. He'd probably used the last of his strength to shift and tell me that.

Fuck.

What about Ivy? What about Xander?

I reached for my phone but realized I'd never grabbed it from upstairs after bringing Cole in. I shut the door to the room and grabbed a blanket, wrapped it around Cole, and lifted him into my arms. There was no way I was leaving him.

Dante was probably waiting for the opportune moment to finish the job and kill him. I couldn't let that happen.

Hopeful there wasn't an ambush waiting for me in the den, I walked as quickly as possible through the tunnel and cracked the door, peeking out. It was empty, but that didn't mean whoever was working with Dante wasn't waiting.

He had to have help to pull something like this off. I would kill them all. This was treason.

Opening the door all the way, I focused on not freaking out. I could make it to the truck and get us the hell out of this situation. I just needed to get there without being seen and we'd be golden.

Stopping at the door leading out to the front, I wished there was glass in the door so I could see out. In my head, I imagined two dozen men with automatic weapons keeping a perimeter around the house.

The metal door creaked as I opened it, and I paused, waiting to see if the boogie man was going to jump out at me. Nothing happened, and I poked my head out, listening carefully. Our senses in human form weren't nearly as great as when we were wolfed out.

As soon as I was out the door, Ivy's scent hit me, and I nearly dropped Cole and fell to my knees.

Fear.

A growl threatened to escape, and my canines extended at the idea of my mate being scared. *Get Cole in the truck and hidden, then look for her.* The pep talk to myself helped, and I steeled my spin and grip on Cole.

Dashing across the lawn to the driveway, I was just about to open the door to the truck when something hard and metal pressed into the back of my head.

"And where do you think you're going?" Brian, one of Dante's buddies, kept what I quickly realized was a gun, pressed to my head as he moved to the side so I could see him. "Put him down."

Baring my teeth, I didn't at first, but then he dug the barrel of the gun into my scalp. He was going to kill me, and then I'd be no good to Cole or Ivy. Oh, God. Where was Xander? He had to be freaking out.

Squatting carefully, I set Cole on the gravel and stood with my hands up in surrender. I needed to think of a plan, and quick.

An ATV started up in the garage, and a few moments later, Dante pulled out with Ivy strapped to the back. Her legs were tied and a muzzle was on her. I didn't even think, lunging forward to get to her, but Brian grabbed me from behind and threw me to the ground.

The urge to shift was strong, but I pushed my wolf back. They wouldn't hesitate to shoot me in my wolf form. At least with me still being human, they might think twice.

I stood slowly, my body burning from hitting the rough gravel. "What are you doing?"

Dante threw his head back and laughed. Had he lost his mind? "Just going for a little evening drive with my gal, Ivy."

Growls came from the side of the house, and three wolves bounded around the corner. Brian and Dante didn't hesitate, and I fell to my knees as three of the pack's strongest males besides the betas were shot.

Brian held his gun against my head again, the barrel hot to the touch. The smell of blood filled the air, and I looked away from the scene in front of me.

"Now, here are your choices, Omega." Dante got off the ATV, leaving it running. "You can either comply or end up painting the driveway my new favorite color. The place could use a little redecoration."

When I didn't answer, he pistol whipped me, my mouth filling with blood and my face burning from the hit. I spat toward his boots, a tooth flying with the blood, but it came up short, which only made him laugh.

He squatted down, a smirk twisting his face into something sinister. "You know, maybe I *should* kill you, and then your sweet little sister can take her rightful place on her knees in front of me... and under me."

Nausea churned inside my stomach at the thought of him getting his hands on Sara. "Fuck you."

He shoved the gun under my chin and lifted it until I was looking down my nose at him. "I think I'll make you watch."

I couldn't stop the whimper from escaping, and Dante pistol whipped me again. This time, something cracked inside my head and I fell over, curling into a ball.

"Get Cole and that other mutt locked in the basement." He stood and put his gun back in his holster. "Tie this one up to a chair in the kitchen and please, for the love of the moon, find his fucking sister."

I attempted to crawl after Dante but then pain exploded in my head as a boot pressed it into the ground. I was helpless as I watched Dante drive away with my mate lying limp, tied up like an animal on the back of the ATV.

CHAPTER TWENTY-NINE

Silas

"*Alpha!*" Bone's irritating voice pulled me from my sleep. The fucker always woke me up after a hard night, and I was about ready to rip his throat out. He was perfectly capable as my top beta to handle any situation.

"*What?*" Sometimes I wondered why I didn't just close the connection. It was a pain in the ass.

"*You need to get out to the river.*" He sounded panicked. I groaned and threw the sheet off of me.

Rolling out of bed, I landed on my hands and knees and tried to shake off the hangover I was sporting. I climbed to my feet and grabbed my pants off the floor but nearly fell over putting them on.

Wolves processed alcohol differently, but when you

drink an entire bottle of Jack in a short period of time, it will fuck you up.

"*What's wrong?*" It was probably something stupid, like a dead animal or a colony of beavers that set up a dam.

"*It's a female wolf. She smells like the one that's been staying with Cole's pack. The redhead.*"

Well, I'd be damned. My bunny had come to her wolf at last.

"*Don't you touch her! I'm on my way!*"

After pulling my pants back off, I opened the door to my bedroom and shuffled onto the landing overlooking the large den area where we spent most of our time as a pack. It was pretty quiet since it was a weekday and everyone had work.

I ran down the steps and to the door. Springing forward, I shifted and nearly took down Bone in my haste to get to her. I fucking knew I should have just thrown her on the back of my bike the first time I met her.

"*We need to get her back to the den. She's in bad shape,*" Rover, my second beta, said.

"*What do you mean? I'll be there in a minute.*" The river was close, and I sprinted across the yard and into the trees.

"*They tied her up and muzzled her.*"

The growl that came from me was unlike anything I'd experienced. If she died, I was going to rip Cole's dick off, shove it down his throat, then rip his head off and shove it up his ass.

I burst from the trees, and then I saw her.

My mate.

I shifted and dropped to my knees beside her lifeless body. "Bunny." I felt for a pulse, but it was weak. "Fuck! Give me your shirt!"

Rover ripped off his flannel shirt, sending buttons flying, and handed me it. I didn't like the idea of his scent being on her, but she was soaking wet and freezing.

Wrapping the shirt around her, I picked her up as carefully as possible and ran back to the den.

Why would they do this to her?

"How did you find her?" I could barely speak with my canines being out from my anger. I was going to kill them. Every last one of them.

"Found her tangled up in some debris on the shore. She was bound with ropes and a muzzle. As soon as we saw her we called for you." Bone looked more worried than I liked, and I growled at him, causing him to increase the space between us.

When I first met her and knew she was my mate, I should have grabbed her and taken her. How did I know Cole could be so heartless? He was a fucking saint while I was the sinner. One thing was for sure, he wouldn't be getting his paws on her or any other female ever again.

"Get ready to ride." I took my bunny straight into the den and up the stairs. She needed a warm bed and rest.

"Alpha?" Bone looked up at me as I stopped on the landing. "How many reinforcements do you want me to alert?"

"All of them. We're going to war." I looked down at the limp red wolf in my arms. She was exquisite with hair speckled with red and golden hues. "No one fucks with my mate."

TO BE CONTINUED...

Printed in Great Britain
by Amazon